Walking Wounded

To Larry—
I hope these stories
ring true for you.
Bon Chance

Carl Owen

December, 2006

Walking Wounded

STORIES

Jimmy Carl Harris

Iris Press
Oak Ridge, Tennessee

Copyright © 2006 by Jimmy Carl Harris

Iris Press

www.irisbooks.com

Cover Painting © 2006 by Deborah Ann Cidboy

Design: Robert B. Cumming, Jr.

Library of Congress Cataloging-in-Publication Data

Harris, Jimmy Carl.
Walking wounded : stories / Jimmy Carl Harris.
    p. cm.
ISBN-13: 978-0-916078-71-3 (alk. paper)
ISBN-10: 0-916078-71-X (alk. paper)
ISBN-13: 978-0-916078-72-0 (pbk. : alk. paper)
ISBN-10: 0-916078-72-8 (pbk. : alk. paper)
I. Title.
PS3608.A7829W35 2006
813'.6—dc22

                                          2006012691

Acknowledgments

To all who said I could when I was sure I couldn't. To my Hindman family, probably the best support group there ever was. To the Smoke City Narrators, who made me see what I had to see. To Deb Klaus, a loyal friend. To Sandy Tritt, a constant mentor. To Deb Cidboy, whose creative spirit embraces this book from cover to cover. To the walking wounded, who permitted me to tell some of their stories and to tell them in my way.

Some of these stories have appeared, often in a slightly different form or under a different title, in *The Louisville Review, Byline Magazine, Appalachian Heritage, Confluence, The Tulane Review, Serpentine,* or *The Birmingham Arts Journal.* All of these stories have been successful in contests, including the Hackney Literary Award and honors bestowed by the Southeastern Writers Association, Southwest Writers, Alabama Writers Conclave, Tennessee Mountain Writers, and Appalachian Writers Association.

To all who wake up tired but go to work,
who wake up hurt but fix breakfast anyway,
who wake up afraid but keep on keeping on.
To the walking wounded.

Contents

The Communists of My Youth

I was three days in-country and it was the middle of the night. Somebody yelled "Sappers in the wire." Tracers were going every which way. Sergeant Tavares took off toward the perimeter. I followed, bumped into a shadow, lost my M-16. There were muzzle flashes and Sgt. T went down. His feet began to dig and push, then the air went out of him and he was still. Somebody popped an illumination flare and I looked around for help. There was a sapper ten yards away, leaning against the communications bunker. His black shirt glistened wet below his throat. He and Sgt. T had shot each other.

The flare floated above us, washing us with its ghost-light, the dead, the dying, the wounded forever. The sapper's grin, pain plus hate, was directed at me. He lifted his weapon and cranked off a short burst that took me center-mass, slammed into my flak jacket. I landed on my butt in the mud and began to fade. Victor Charlie slid down the sandbag wall of the bunker. His AK-47 wavered left, right, down. He screamed some angry word, then used the last of his life trying to kill me. Something jerked at my left foot and I passed out.

Every spring, Mr. Nelson would present his World History students with this little book he'd written in college. The assignment was to read and discuss it, then take a test. Sandra Hulett, who liked me at the same time I liked Mignon Capps, told me it was a big deal to have a teacher who'd written a book and I caught on. I asked enough questions to get in trouble with my classmates and I made a B+ on the test, the highest grade I made during four years at Nall County High.

The point of Mr. Nelson's thesis was that communism started out to be the salvation of the Russians, and maybe the world, but ended up an evil thing. Millions of Russians died and communism spread all over the world in an effort to destroy democracy and the American way of life. Mr. Nelson had a dramatic way of demonstrating what the Vietnam War was about. He'd get out a box of dominoes and set them up the way little kids do, on end and an inch apart, in a row. He'd name the first domino Russia, the second China. Further down the chain was North Korea, then Vietnam. Next, he'd put a record on his old portable and announce that the *Internationale* is the anthem of international communism. Then, with the music playing, he'd push the first domino over and click, click, down they'd go. He'd pick up the last fallen domino and say "America."

That, and how to run a slant pass pattern and how to french inhale and how to unsnap a bra with one hand, was about all I learned in high school. When I told Mr. Nelson I was going into the Marine Corps, he said he was sorry he'd not had the privilege of serving, but he'd had poor eyesight. He said I'd be in the front lines of the struggle with international communism, and I could be proud of that.

Was I dead or alive? I concentrated on opening my eyes. If I was alive, I'd be in the muck of Con Thien and there'd be a dead communist. If I was dead, there'd be the face of God. I got my eyes half open. Light, brighter than any flare, was coming from everywhere. A tall man, dressed all in white, was standing beside me. I was dead. God nodded and turned away. It was Judgment Day.

I closed my eyes and waited to hear the angels sing. There was no heavenly music. Maybe I'd been sent to hell, so I opened my eyes again. Thank God, there was an angel. The angel was wearing a navy nurse uniform. She looked like she could bite through a twenty-penny nail, or break down and cry, or both. She placed a cool, hard hand on my forehead and said "Welcome back, Marine."

The Veterans Administration puts you close to home, if they can, so I ended up back in Alabama. It didn't matter to me. My folks were killed in a car wreck when I was six and the uncle who raised me died while I was in boot camp. But, the VA meant well. They sent me to the hospital in Tuscaloosa because the one in Birmingham had a full quota of one-legged Marines. The VA folks tried to convince me I was lucky because I still had one whole leg and most of the other, including a knee that still worked. I didn't feel all that lucky but they had a point. With the prosthesis they gave me, within six months I could hobble around pretty good, even got to where I could work the clutch for a stick shift. The VA discharge counselor suggested that, since the University of Alabama was across town, I should take advantage of the GI Bill and go to college.

I let him take me to the campus, where everybody had two beautiful legs and looked like they were glad of it. After one hour of being felt sorry for, I told the VA guy I had a better idea. He was a pretty good guy, in that he helped me with my plan and never tried to talk me out of it.

What I did was, I collected my back pay and bought a used ten-wide which was already set up on a red-dirt lot up in Nall County, about a mile off the state route to Ebenezer and near a played-out strip mine. It was furnished, more or less, good enough for my purpose. My plan was to sit out there, in the woods, and figure out life. I planned to drink a lot of beer while I figured.

But, before I went to the woods, there was Chuck LeGrande.

I was in the day room, playing bingo, when one of the tenders came with a wheelchair. I was already walking well enough to not need the ride, but he insisted and wheeled me into the front lobby. His explanation was that some big shot wanted to meet me. I'd already been interviewed by my hometown newspaper in connection with Decoration Day, so I figured this was more of the same. While I waited, a guy in a blue suit came in the front door and started sitting up lights and a big movie-style camera on tripods. I asked him what the hell was happening. He said I was going to be on television with Chuck LeGrande.

When you're sitting around the VA, waiting for your turn at physical therapy, you have plenty of time to read newspapers. That, or just sit and stare out the window, like some did. I chose reading over staring, so I'd heard of Brigadier General Charles Edward LeGrande, United States Army Retired, the candidate of the Patriots Party for President of the United States of America. I knew his campaign slogan was "Better Dead than Red."

BlueSuit plugged in his lights and I was blinded. He ordered me to keep my mouth shut, said the general would do the talking. Marine PFCs are used to being told what to do, so I did. Through the glare, I saw BlueSuit step behind the camera. We waited.

A hand dropped onto my shoulder. By squinting sideways, I could see that it was attached to a large man standing beside me. He cleared his throat, then declared, in a Fourth of July voice, "Young men like this one sacrificed themselves to protect America from the godless communists. To honor these heroes,

I will continue the fight." After that, he said something about where to send contributions. He repeated his little speech, this time in a Thanksgiving voice, then walked out the front door and got into a black Cadillac. BlueSuit was still disassembling his equipment when the handler carted me away.

Two days later, BlueSuit came back. This time, there was no camera and no general, so they let me clip-clop to the day room on my own, no wheels. BlueSuit said the hospital director was going to release me and some other heroes to the Chuck LeGrande campaign. He smirked when he said "Heroes," but I didn't think much of being called that, either. I tried to pump BlueSuit for more information, but the most he'd say was "You'll find out." Although I was about to be released, anyway—I'd already signed the papers for my trailer—the Marine in me figured this was something I had to do because somebody who outranked me said so.

There were three of us. The oldest, Arnold, a black guy from up North, had been an army tanker. He'd gotten his hands burned off when he snatched a white phosphorous grenade away from a fifty gallon drum of gasoline. The VA rigged him up with some metal claws, scary looking things. The Mexican-American, Jesus, also ex-army, had been a door gunner until a surface-to-air missile took his helicopter down. For that, he got an Air Medal and a free trip to Alabama and a mostly plastic face. And, there was me, the leg-and-a-half white Marine. There wasn't anyone from the navy or the air force, probably because they mostly had some college and were smart enough not to get suckered into this cockamamie project.

Arnold said a paraplegic left over from Korea told him Chuck LeGrande had been a passed-over captain at the beginning of World War Two and would have been forced out of the army, except for the war. He spent the entire war in Washington, DC, sucking up to politicians and getting promoted. During the Korean War, he was back in Washington, writing reports about the communist threat. In the mid-fifties, some senator with a hard-on for the communists made him a brigadier general. Arnold said this deal was still better than hanging around in the VA, even if ol' Chuck was a phony. I didn't argue with Arnold, but I figured nobody made brigadier without having something on the ball.

Our job was to sit on the stage behind General LeGrande while he made the exact same speech eight or ten times a day. He'd come on stage, wearing khaki trousers and a khaki bush jacket—Jesus called it his Jungle Jim get-up—and commence to speechify about sacrifice. At the end, while the loudspeakers blared out "God Bless America," he'd salute each of us. When Arnold returned the salute with his right claw, even white folks in the audience would get misty-eyed. Then, some local preacher'd ask God to bless us and we'd be back on the bus and off to another one-horse town in another of the dusty states. We did all our campaigning between the Mississippi River and the Rocky Mountains because, as BlueSuit explained to us, Nixon was from California, the yankees would mostly go for Humphrey, and Wallace was coming on strong with his Segregation Forever thing in the South. BlueSuit said it was pretty damned funny, how the other three would be weakened by fighting amongst themselves, while LeGrande got a toe-hold in places like the Dakotas. From that base, he expected to take enough veteran votes from the others for a long-shot win.

The general rode in the Cadillac and stayed in motels with swimming pools. The Purple Heart Posse slept on the bus, with BlueSuit there to keep us from running off. About two weeks out, somewhere north of Pierre, Arnold got up the nerve to ask our candidate why he thought it was that people would vote for him instead of the others. Ol' Chuck invited us over to his Holiday Inn so he could give us a pep-talk about his vision. He sat down with the three of us beside the pool and, for about

ten minutes, spoke directly to us for the only time in the month
we were together. He said we'd been wounded while fighting
international communism, which wanted to enslave us—he
looked at Arnold—and burn our churches—he looked at Jesus
who, being a Mexican, was therefore a Catholic. He said he
was the only true warrior of democracy running for president.
He leaned forward, looked me in the eye, and said we were
together on a freedom crusade. Then, he stood up and told us
it had been a long day, we all needed some sleep.

I believed everything the general told us. Even when the
Nixon people released his entire military record, including the
part about no combat. Even after the bank tracked us down and
took the bus, and I had to pay my own way back to Alabama,
I still believed him. Maybe it was because it was the biggest
thing a nineteen-year-old from a county with one traffic light
had ever been a part of. I accepted the general's idea that my
war and his campaign were directly connected. I'd been face-
to-face with communism and I believed him.

There was another trailer on the other side of the kudzu patch
that was slowly swallowing my lot. Occasionally, I'd see a man,
small, white-haired, step out of the trailer and go around to the
back of it. He never hollered, never waved, never even looked
my way. Without a word passing between us, we had a deal—
I'll stay out of your business, you stay out of mine.

Then, about a month after I settled in, I saw some smoke,
which looked like it was coming out of one end of my neighbor's
trailer. Because I was well into my late breakfast of beer and
potato chips, it took a while for me to decide I ought to do
something. I still had enough sense not to try to wade through
the kudzu, so I went out to the dirt road that connected both of
us to the blacktop, then around to the smoldering trailer.

His trailer was about the same age and size as mine. Except

for the new double-wides, they all look pretty much alike, narrow boxes made of thin, white aluminum, two feet above the dirt on cinder-block columns. When I got there, I saw that the smoke was coming from behind the trailer rather than from inside it. So, I stiff-legged my way around the trailer, cautious, checking it out.

On the other side of his trailer was a little trash fire that had spread to some dead weeds. That, and my neighbor trying to push a car away from the fire and toward a shed. It was a 1950 Mercury two-door, the James Dean kind, sleek, black, low-slung. He was looking over his shoulder at me, so I helped him. Then, we got after the fire, him with an old piece of blanket and me kicking dirt, which must look pretty funny when it's done by a peg-leg.

After the fire was out, he nodded at me, said "Much obliged," and offered me a Camel.

I'd left my Marlboros in my trailer, so I accepted the smoke, pulled out my lighter, and lit both cigarettes. "Been living here for a while?"

He took a long draw on his cigarette. "Year, maybe."

"Where'd you come from?"

He looked directly at me and waited for a long moment. "Long way from here." He shifted his eyes to the Mercury. "Got to get busy." He moved toward the car.

"Well, see you later."

He nodded, then dropped to one knee and began inspecting a rear wheel.

I needed at least sixteen cases of beer to make it through two months. It was cheaper to buy beer and cigarettes on base, but each base places a limit on such purchases. So, every other month, soon as I got my medical retirement check, I'd fire up my GMC pickup at dawn and take off on a 400 mile circuit of the nearest bases, Selma and Meridian and Columbus. Whatever was left of my income after I bought the necessary stuff, I'd spend on food. I made a supply run the month after the fire. On impulse, I bought an extra carton of cigarettes, Camels. I was too worn out to deliver them when I got back, so I went over the next day. I knocked for a while, then left the cigarettes on his doorstep.

I went back the next day and the cigarettes were gone. I still couldn't raise anybody, so I went around the house and stood looking at the Mercury. It was in pretty good shape—good paint, decent tires, no dents. Because there was still some teenage boy left in me, I popped the hood. The engine was covered with a greasy rag, which I lifted. He'd removed the carburetor, intake and exhaust manifolds, and cylinder heads.

"I'm going to soup it up." He'd come out of the woods. He was wearing a faded brown hunter's jacket, heavy cotton twill with loops for shotgun shells across the chest and a game pouch in the back. In one hand he held a single-shot twenty-gauge.

He saw I was staring at his shotgun. "Squirrels."

I nodded about the squirrels, then I nodded toward the Mercury. "Hard to get speed equipment for a flathead."

"Yeah. Thanks for the cigarettes." He reached into the game pouch and pulled out two dead squirrels. "You up to some squirrel and dumplings?"

During the whole time he was cleaning the squirrels and making the dumplings, he said not a word. I've always respected a man who's serious about his work, so I just sat at his little kitchen table and watched. Once he'd finished the interesting blood and guts part, my attention wandered. I wished I had a beer but he'd not offered me one and I didn't want to sound desperate by asking.

I'd noticed a couple of pictures on the wall when we came in, so I got up and took a look. I figure, if a man puts pictures on his wall, it's his way of telling you who he is. Both pictures were of about a dozen men in their twenties or thirties, different men but wearing similar uniforms—faded, too-large trousers, dark-colored shirts that looked as though they were newly-issued, odds-and-ends caps that ranged from seaman to infantry.

In each picture, the men fell into two categories. Some had their caps cocked to one side and looked as though they were laughing at the camera. The others were slouched and seemed to be looking beyond the camera at something they'd rather not see. Those in the picture captioned "Civilian Conservation Corps, Camp Hill," had shovels and hoes and picks slung over their shoulders. The men in the picture labeled "Lincoln Battalion, Teruel," also had their tools in hand, but their tools were bolt-action Mausers.

The squirrel pot bubbled away, producing an aroma that made my mouth water, while my host mixed and rolled and cut the dumplings. Once he dropped them in, it was only a few minutes before we could eat. He put two steaming bowls on the table and we made use of the salt and pepper shakers. His silence, and mine, continued until the food was gone.

I pushed away from the table and stifled a belch. "Good chow." I wondered if there was any connection between the pictures and the scar above his right eye. I wanted to ask, but he'd seen me looking at the pictures and said nothing. So, I left it alone. We smoked a cigarette and exchanged a few comments about the weather. I got up to leave.

"Thanks again for the smokes."

Two months later, I brought him another carton of Camels and a case of Budweiser. This time, after I knocked, I sat on a stump and waited. I'd brought along a six-pack for myself, so I had something to do. After about half an hour, the door opened. He stepped over his gifts and stood in the yard for maybe a minute, looking at me. He looked discombobulated, maybe a hangover, maybe something else. He also looked like he'd lost some weight, and he'd been small to begin with.

"I heard you knock, but I had to lay down for a while. Come on in." He turned around, picked up his beer and cigarettes, and went back inside.

Since I had half a six-pack in my hand, I offered him one. Because he was a Camel smoker, it surprised me that he shook his head in refusal. On the other hand, he kept the case of beer I'd brought him. He opened the door of his refrigerator and, with both hands on its top, leaned over and peered into it. "I got some left-over meat loaf and I could fry some potatoes. That okay with you?"

I said that was fine by me. I sat down and opened one of my beers. He put the meat loaf in the oven and cut up some potatoes and onions. Potatoes and onions frying smell almost as good as squirrel and dumplings, and don't take nearly as long. I held off on conversation until we began eating. "My uncle was in the CCC."

He nodded toward the pictures. "So was I."

"I saw that. I was in the Marine Corps."

"Figured something like that."

I leaned over and gave my prosthesis a good knuckle-rap. "AK-47. Con Thien. 1967. Third Battalion, Ninth Marines."

He ran a fingertip along the scar above his eyebrow. "Mortar. Jarama. 1937. Lincoln Battalion." He stabbed a piece of potato with his fork and started to put it in his mouth, then paused. "You know anywhere to get speed equipment?"

"Probably find a place in Birmingham."

"If I give you the money, reckon you could run down there? I'd pay for your gas."

The Mercury was the other thing about him I found interesting, so I agreed to make the trip. As soon as we finished eating, he gave me a list—Edelbrock dual intake manifold,

Stromberg carburetors, Offenhauser high compression heads, Mallory ignition, complete dual exhaust system with Smitty steel-packed mufflers. He wanted the best and gave me a thousand dollars to make sure I had enough.

The day before I went to Birmingham, I drove down to Tuscaloosa and went to the University of Alabama library. I could've gone to the Nall County Library in Ebenezer, but I figured I needed something bigger and better. After I thrashed around for a while, I spotted a girl behind a counter, beneath an information sign. Her nametag declared her to be Hadley. My first thought was that Hadley sounds like a boy's name. My second thought was that her shoulders were broader than some boy's. It's not that she was unattractive—she looked okay, in a library assistant sort of way. It was more like she didn't care, judging by her hair, which just hung there, and her makeup, of which there wasn't any, and her faded sweatshirt, which hid any girlness it might contain.

"May I help you with something?" She sounded better than she looked. A lot of people behind counters, when they ask you that question, they sound like they don't really want to help but they have to ask. Hadley had life in her eyes and an honest smile.

"Please. I need to know something about history stuff. I guess." My face got hot and probably red as a beet but Hadley was studying the list I'd handed her.

"Goodness. This is certainly an eclectic list. American laborers in the Spanish Civil War—is that the unifying theme?"

I had no idea what eclectic meant and I'd never heard of the Spanish Civil War. My first inclination was to say something smart-aleck to cover my ignorance. I probably would have, except that the openness of her face told me it wasn't a put-down. She thought I was a student and was simply treating me as an equal. But, that had to be dealt with. "I'm not a student here. I just thought y'all could help me with this."

"This library is open to the community. I'm glad to help." She came from behind the counter and headed toward a long wooden cabinet with hundreds of little drawers. Halfway there, she glanced back at me, smiled, and said "Come with me."

I backed my GMC up to the Mercury and dropped the tailgate. I helped him pile the parts on a bench at the far end of the shed. Then, after he coughed his way through lighting a cigarette, I handed him a receipt and counted out his change.

He looked at the receipt. "You didn't take out gas money."

"I kept my promise. I don't want your money."

He studied my face for a moment, then shrugged and turned toward his trailer.

"I found out some things about those pictures on your wall."

He stopped and turned to face me. "And?"

"In Spain, you were in the International Brigade?"

"Yes."

"They were communists?"

"Syndicalists, anarchists, communists, socialists, democrats, you name it."

"You one of them?"

He returned to where I was standing. Before I could stop him, he stuffed a twenty into my shirt pocket. "That ought to cover your gas and time." He headed toward his trailer.

I followed him. "My uncle never would've been in the CCC with communists."

Again, he faced me. "Don't know that I ever met the man, so I can't speak for him. The Civilian Conservation Corps tried to make things better for the common people. The International

Brigade fought for the same thing. Some men gave their sweat for the CCC and their blood for the Republic." It was the longest speech I'd ever heard from him.

I'd struggled through several chapters in the books Hadley found for me. I partially understood what he was saying, except that I saw things in a whole different light. I'd read that some of the men who'd been in the CCC had gone on to be labor organizers and some newspapers called them communists. As for the Spanish Republic, the picture that stayed with me was of a foreign-looking man with a hammer and sickle painted on his helmet. "Franklin Delano Roosevelt meant for the CCC to plant trees, not communism. After the CCC, my uncle was in the miner's union, but he was never a red. Matter of fact, he was a Mason."

He kept moving while I talked, going back into the shed, removing one of the Strombergs from its carton and turning it around and around in his hands. "Roosevelt did right, up to a point. Your uncle was probably a good union man. Let's leave it there."

I wasn't ready to. "Vietnam never wanted to be a communist domino, and that's how I ended up a peg-leg." I deliberately made my voice louder. "I helped out on Chuck LeGrande's campaign, which was about making a sacrifice for the American way of life." The LeGrande spiel sounded ridiculous, coming from me, but I was not about to back down before a communist.

He jammed the carburetor into its carton and tossed it onto the bench. "LeGrande's a coward. You desecrated your own courage for the ambitions of a fascist." This time, when he stalked away, he did not stop.

It could hardly be called a date, just cheeseburgers and cokes and talking about my neighbor. Hadley listened for awhile, then interrupted. "He sounds like a man who stands up for what he believes."

"Standing up for it don't make it right." I wanted Hadley to know that I'd been tricked into befriending a man who held with those I'd been shot by and campaigned against. "Communists make you think they only want to help you, then they take over."

Hadley held up her hand. The flash of argument in her eyes gave way to something else, something sad but also cold. "He's alone and lonely. He needs a friend, not a judge. We all need that." She stood up, leaving part of her cheeseburger uneaten. "I'll just walk back to the library."

The next month, on my supply run, I loaded up on Camels. My idea was to not actually say anything to him, just leave the cigarettes on his door step and see what happened. Maybe he'd wave or even come over to my trailer. We'd get to talking about the Mercury and just stay away from politics. But, it was threatening to rain so I decided against leaving the cigarettes outside. There was no answer to my knock, but the door was unlocked and I stepped inside.

I remembered the smell from my first day in-country, when I was on a burial detail for a VC who'd been hanging in our wire for a couple of days. Heavy, putrid, the odor clogged my nostrils and made my stomach flip. He was on his bed, dressed in his hunting jacket, his arms wrapped around his shotgun, like they'd laid down together for a nap. The blood this time was dried past glistening, but it had the same dark finality as that of the sapper.

I needed something to stop my stomach from churning so I went to the refrigerator. On top of the case of beer he'd kept for me was an unsealed letter. I guess he figured that, when I found him, I'd want a beer.

He said anybody who smoked on top of lung cancer deserved what he got. He said he was sorry about the mess he'd probably left, but he'd rather pull the plug himself and not have to rot away. He said he had no regrets about who he'd been or what he'd done. He said he had no family, so I could have anything I wanted. It surprised me to see that he knew my full name—I didn't recall ever telling him that. At the bottom, above his signature, were the words *No Pasaran*. With the note was the pink slip for the Mercury, transferring ownership to me.

I keep the Mercury in the garage, along with the Cherokee and the boat. The twenty gauge, I gave to our oldest son. He loves to tell its story to our Republican friends at the country club. Once a month, I take the Mercury out for some exercise. I always tell Hadley I'm going to swing by the campus to check my e-mail, maybe grade some papers, maybe run some errands around Tuscaloosa. She always smiles and says that's good, she has some papers of her own to grade.

After I cross into Nall County, the traffic thins. The weight of thirty years has caused the trailers to collapse into themselves. They're blanketed over—the kudzu finally won, as it always does. It don't mean nothing. My pilgrimages are more of sound than sight. The Mercury is from the radio-only days, so I always bring a portable tape player. I click a cassette into the player and turn the volume up. I double-clutch down into second and floor it. The howl of the Strombergs sucking air and the deep-throated rumble of the exhaust blend with the *Internationale* and echo among the pines.

Hot and Sunny On the Fourth

Hot woke up resolved to do something about it. She fixed herself some eggs, then took to the trail that began at her back door and climbed up to the clearest air. She sat on a fallen sycamore beside the trail and thought it through. With her mind settled on what needed to be done, she returned home and put on the necessary clothes. She went out to her truck and ground the starter until it coughed itself awake.

It was midmorning when Hot came down off the mountain. She thought of it as her mountain and was grateful the strip miners had determined it contained too little coal to justify ripping it apart with bulldozers. An early rain had left a ground fog that swirled around the hurrying truck and tried to embrace it like a cool shroud. Near the point where the narrow blacktop curved around an outcrop of ancient rock, an alert doe nudged her curious offspring away from the roadside. The guttural exhaust echoed up the hollow and startled blue jays so they bolted for a higher limb.

Hot slowed when she reached the spot where, in April, a category four tornado had dipped its angry funnel into the hollow and reduced Macedonia Full Gospel Holiness to widely dispersed kindling. She remembered the old church, its bare wood pews worn slick by generations. There, on a chilly October day thirty years back, a teenage girl, not yet called Hot, came forward and accepted Christ as her personal savior. The preacher took her the next Sunday at dawn to be washed free of sin by full immersion in the icy creek that ran behind the church.

In 1951, six years after she'd been baptized in the name
of the Father, the Son, and the Holy Ghost, she returned
from a sojourn up in Nashville. On her first Sunday back, she
slipped into a back pew. Throughout the sermon, she endured
being glanced at by red-faced men and glared at by hard-eyed
women. She left during the invitational hymn and never came
back. Still, from then on, if anyone had bothered to ask, she
would have claimed membership in the church where she had
professed her faith.

Today, Hot saw that several men from the congregation had
worked up a good sweat preparing the surviving foundation for
a new white frame church identical to the old one. She glanced
at the graveyard they had cleared of debris on Decoration Day.
She noted the recent graves, the eternal resting places of the
four souls whose trailer had been found by the twister. She'd
heard, during one of her infrequent trips into Ebenezer, that
the adults were found huddled where the bathroom had been
but the baby was taken up by the heartless wind and dropped
into the creek. She thought of stopping to inquire about a burial
plot but decided against it. There'd be time enough later for
dealing with last rites. She rumbled on down toward town.

At the intersection with County Route Four, Hot pressed
her palm against the steering wheel and spun it in a sharp
turn toward Ebenezer. She released the wheel, punched the
accelerator, allowed the pickup to pull itself straight. She
slammed the gearshift up into second right when her own
voice, singing about a lonesome burning soul, spilled out of the
speakers. She dropped the shifter hard into third and continued
to hold the gas pedal to the bare metal floor.

Her lonesome soul number had been the A side of her demo
disk, her get outta this place song the B side. After two years of
being just another mountain girl with haunts in her voice and no
connections, reality had driven Hot out of Nashville. The bus
had dropped her off in Ebenezer. She'd hitchhiked and walked,

trudged the way a woman great with child will, up the hollow to the mountain. Back then, her mamaw was still alive and Hot moved in with her. Hot had lived there ever since, raised her son in the unpainted clapboard house with a splash of yellow jonquils to challenge the shadows cast by the upreaching pines. She'd hid her record in a box of quilting scraps. Only recently, she'd had her sides transferred to an eight-track. She'd told the guy making the tape to fill it out with cheating love songs borrowed from Patsy and the rest.

About half-way between the church and Ebenezer, at the point where the valley began to broaden and modest dwellings were more frequent, was the American Kwik Sak. The small, green-painted cinder block building was surrounded by coils of concertina wire and had an entranceway constructed of neatly piled sandbags. Over the door were crossed flags, one the red, white and blue, the other the three red stripes on yellow of the Republic of Vietnam.

Hot parked outside the wire. She passed between the sandbag walls and under the flags. She looked around the small convenience store, then called out. "Wheels?"

"Back here. Who's that?"

"Hot. I see you got you some of that coiled-up barbed wire."

A legless man in a wheelchair trundled from behind a display of potato chips. His hair was pulled tight back into a ponytail. He was wearing blue jean cut-offs and a sleeveless, camouflage pattern hunting vest. Attached to one side of his wheelchair was a rifle scabbard encasing a battered but well-oiled Winchester Model 74. "Concertina. Man can't be too careful with his security."

"You expecting an invasion?"

Wheels propelled himself to a point where his bare stumps were six inches from Hot. "Yeah. By my own government."

Hot glanced at the pink, withered remains jutting toward

her but held her ground. "Maybe you ought to pay your taxes."

"Maybe I should've gone to Canada. Wha'cha need, Hot Stuff?"

"Smokes."

Wheels spun his chair, rolled behind the counter, and tossed her a red pack of Pall Malls. She nabbed the cigarettes in midair with one hand and put her money on the counter.

Wheels looked Hot over more carefully. "Love your get-up. Where you headed?"

"Ebenezer. Got to tend to some unfinished business."

Wheels looked out the barred window of his store for a long moment. "Sunny."

Hot was already at the door, silhouetted against the glare. She answered before she left. "Sunny."

Wheels lifted a fist to full arm's length and held it there. His shout followed Hot all the way out to her truck. "Right on, Babe, right on."

In Ebenezer, Hot slowed to show respect and pulled into the funeral home parking lot. She quieted the tape and the engine and slid out of her ride. She stood for a moment in front of the ersatz antebellum splendor of the Bondurant Funeral Home, felt the heat of the pavement through the soles of her boots. She field-stripped her cigarette butt, reduced it to tiny shreds of paper and flakes of tobacco, as Wheels had taught her to do. He said it prevented the enemy from knowing where you'd been. She passed between the white columns and shoved the door open.

Aubrey Bondurant, in gray seersucker, sported a wilted carnation in his lapel. He wafted forth from his office and hovered on the beige carpet, positioned in Hot's path. He uttered something that sounded like, "Kanipye?"

Hot put her hands on her hips. "Say what?"

Aubrey took a deep breath and enunciated, "Can I help you?"

"Where y'all got Sunny?"

Aubrey looked Hot over. He took in her olive drab head rag and her faded black tee shirt with *Walking Dead* stretched across her bosom. He briefly appreciated her denim-encased legs, kept slim by thousands of hours on mountain trails, but winced at the sight of her heavy, polished boots. "You're here for the gentleman the VA brought in?"

"Yeah. Sunny."

Confusion joined the resentment puckering Aubrey's round face. "The VA rep said his name was—"

Hot's interruption drove Aubrey back a step. "When he was little, people said he could light up a cloudy day. They took to calling him Sunny and it stuck. Where y'all got him?"

Aubrey flapped a hand toward a door on one side of the lobby. "The Liberty Chapel. We use it for our veterans." He retreated to his paneled cubicle and his muted television set in time to catch the end of the daytime drama he'd been watching.

Hot strode into the chapel. She paused to adjust her eyes to the gloom, then studied the metal cart where the flag-draped coffin rested. She released the brake on each wheel and pushed the cart out of the chapel. She was maneuvering it through the front door when Aubrey reemerged from his office.

Aubrey was instantly breathless. "What're you doing?"

"Something that should've been done a long time ago."

"You can't just remove the deceased from the premises."

"Watch me."

Aubrey grabbed the push bar of the glass front door. He let go when Hot drop-kicked him in the crotch. He squirmed on the carpet, holding himself, while Hot loaded Sunny into the bed of her pickup. She stretched a rope across the truck bed and knotted it into place so that it secured the flag atop the coffin. She rested her hand on the coffin for a moment, then got into her truck.

The courthouse square was early-afternoon quiet. The Fourth of July sun had driven most sensible citizens to seek some shade or, if they were wiser, some recently air-conditioned space. That evening, the square would fill with families half-listening to overweight men in their fifties ramble on about the good war, about Guadalcanal and Anzio. Parents would still their children with promises of Methodist ice cream and Baptist fireworks. The combined church choir, in harmony for the only time of the year, would belt out a fair-to-middling a cappella rendition of "God Bless America."

Hot slowed when she reached the square. She took her tape out of the player and inserted another. The *I Feel Like I'm Fixin' to Die Rag* blasted raucous into the still heat. She circled the courthouse until the patrol units blocked her front and rear.

"Come outta there, Hot." The sheriff's deputy stood ten feet away from Hot's truck, his right thumb hooked in his gun belt. His fingertips dangled near his service revolver.

Hot did as she was told. She leaned against the rear fender of her truck, put fire to a Pall Mall, flicked her Zippo closed with a flourish, and nodded to the deputy. "You won't be needin' your gun, Hank."

Hank bobbed his head in acknowledgment. "I know that." He kept his right hand near his weapon while he waved at Hot with his left. "What's with the get-up?"

Hot gave her head rag a gentle pat and glanced down at her shirt. "This is stuff Sunny brought back from over there." She jerked her head sideways toward the cab of the truck. "The music was his, too."

"I heard it before. In 'Nam. Sorry 'bout Sunny."

Hot took a deep draw on her cigarette and blew a stream

of smoke toward Hank. "What's that y'all said when you got back? 'It don't mean nothing?'"

"Yeah, we said that." Hank tilted his head to one side and looked at Sunny's coffin. "What're you up to, anyway?"

"I'm giving my boy the Fourth of July parade this town never gave him."

Hank laid down the benediction. "Never gave none of us." He came to attention and saluted the mortal remains of the son still in her womb when, more than two decades earlier, she stepped off the bus from Nashville. Then, he asked Hot to please put her hands behind her back.

Rolling Salvation

And there came into the country a man of exceeding beauty and wisdom. He moved among the people of the land, serving them body and soul.

"Whatcha got in there?"

The storekeeper was a slight, fine-featured man with long, wavy light brown hair that would give rise to envy in a woman and suspicion in a man. He searched Mahalie up and down with sweet-smiling eyes. "All manner of things. Goods to please the palate and the pocketbook. Remedies for chigger bites and female problems. Wonders from afar."

Mahalie stood below the entrance to the rolling store, her natural pallor mottled by late July sunburn, her thin figure clad in a hand-me-down dress the Christian Women's Fellowship had dropped off three Christmases back, trying to peer past the storekeeper into the dark interior. The rolling store had only recently appeared in Mahalie's corner of Nall County, Alabama. Essentially, it was a large metal box with one door and no windows, perched on the platform of an old International flatbed. This was the first time she'd waved it down. "Can't see much."

The storekeeper turned sideways. With his outboard hand, he swept more heat into the store. "Well, step right in. There's much to see."

Mahalie hesitated on the lowest step. "All I need is something besides crowder peas and hominy for supper. You got canned goods?"

"Got peaches from Georgia, California figs, pineapple all the way from Hawaii."

"Ottis don't take much to fancy food. Maybe some peaches." Mahalie climbed into the store. The storekeeper flicked a switch, bringing to life a pair of twenty-five watt bulbs and a small oscillating fan. The fan, mounted near the far end of the store and just in front of a faded red curtain, pushed an exotic concoction of smells, nutmeg and tobacco and ripe banana, into Mahalie's face. The storekeeper retreated down the narrow corridor between the laden shelves. He stopped beneath the second bulb and gestured for Mahalie to follow. She did, but paused at a display of lace. "What d'you get for this?"

"Imported from Belgium. On sale at nineteen cents a yard. How much today?"

"Maybe some other time." Mahalie continued into the barely dissipated gloom, past buckets of lard, sacks of Jim Dandy corn meal, jars of Golden Eagle table syrup, spools of thread and packets of needles. She stopped a foot away from the storekeeper. "That your peaches?"

The storekeeper lifted a can and studied it. "Grade A Fancy. Yellow cling in nectar. Very tasty."

Mahalie stood stark-still in the warm wash of pungent air. Despite the scant light, she could see calm and mirth in the storekeeper's dark blue eyes. She offered no resistance to his gaze, felt it soothe her caution and encourage her curiosity. "Not from around here, are you?"

"Originally, I was. Nall County High School, class of '49. Joined the Navy, spent some time in Hong Kong, Singapore, Korea. Got out and went to college in California. Taught school for a while in New Mexico and Hawaii. My papaw passed away and left me this rolling store. End of story. You want the peaches?"

Mahalie nodded and held out a quarter, forcing her eyes to shift to the can of peaches. She noticed that the can was dented but did not complain.

The storekeeper took the quarter from Mahalie and handed her the peaches. He opened a cigar box on the shelf near his elbow, dropped the quarter on top of a couple of dollar bills, and selected some coins from among the several dozen covering the bottom of the box. He took Mahalie's empty hand, gently pressed two dimes into her upturned palm, then curled her fingers over them.

Mahalie took a step back, breaking contact. She opened her hand and frowned at the silver coins. "Cheap."

"Special price for a special customer."

Mahalie turned toward the door. She paused long enough for the tremor in her knees to pass, then took short steps to the door and carefully descended to the road. She stood, her back to the rolling store, looking at but not seeing the fresh zigzag pressed into the dirt. She started when the steps, removed for travel, clanged on the metal floor of the store but was prepared for the slam of the door.

"See you next week. Same day, between eleven and one. We'll talk some more about that lace."

Mahalie did not turn or speak. She waited until the rolling store pulled away, then nodded.

Ottis spent most of his enlistment in the stockade for stealing a gross of doughnuts from the Red Cross and attempting to sell those he did not consume to the USO. He returned to Nall County in late 1954 and entered upon the profession of chicken catcher. His main job was to plod through the chicken house, bent at the waist, snatching up terrified fryers by their ankles and stuffing them into shipping cages. His other important tasks included scraping offal from the floor of the chicken house and building bonfires of the carcasses of dead birds that had succumbed to assorted chicken maladies.

Mahalie, barely seventeen and having been approached only by Ottis, agreed to marry him on the strength of his promise to get a brand new car as soon as he was admitted to the training program at the Bondurant Funeral Parlor. As it turned out, there never was a volume of death that would force the funeral parlor to hire an ex-con with chicken feces under his nails and partially burnt feathers in his hair. By the summer of 1958, Mahalie's dreams of a low, sleek Studebaker had been replaced with nightmares featuring black eyes and split lips.

Mahalie decided to keep the dimes forever. She sewed them into a tiny pouch made from a slightly stained handkerchief and tucked the pouch into a private place. Unfortunately, this meant she had no disposable cash. Nevertheless, she kept an alert eye on calendar and clock and was standing by the mailbox the following week when the rolling store, brakes squealing, halted at her station.

The storekeeper climbed out of the cab and met Mahalie at the back of his vehicle. "Morning, ma'am. Want another look at that lace? I got some left but it's going fast."

"Looking's all I can afford. I'm outa cash."

The storekeeper reached up, opened the door, and dragged the steps out and into position. "Come on in, anyway. Maybe we can talk trade. You got eggs?"

Mahalie remained standing in the road at the bottom of the steps. Indeed, she had eggs. From time to time, Ottis brought home a chicken, not dead but too scrawny to meet the market muster. Some immediately had their necks wrung and went into the pot. Some, Mahalie rescued and nourished to maturity as laying hens. "Reckon I could come up with a dozen."

"Fetch'em. I'll take eggs for lace. I can sell the eggs in Ebenezer. Here's a sack." He handed Mahalie a paper bag.

Mahalie hastened to do his bidding. She raided every nest in the hen house, when necessary plunging a hand beneath a complaining biddy to steal her small brown egg. There were thirteen eggs available and she did not hesitate to place the extra egg in the sack. When she returned to the rolling store, the storekeeper was sitting on the top step with his eyes closed. A yard of cream-colored lace was draped around his neck and he was reading its delicate design with his fingertips. Mahalie stood transfixed, feeling the sweat inching down her thighs, watching the storekeeper caress the lace as though he expected some response from it.

The storekeeper opened his eyes and extended the ends of the lace toward Mahalie. "Straight from Brussels. Turn a pretty girl into an elegant lady. Where you going to wear it?"

"Around here, I guess. I don't go nowhere."

"No, I meant, will you make a collar for your dress or something more intimate?"

Mahalie colored up, a blush darkening her sunburn. She shrugged, then offered the eggs to the storekeeper. "There's thirteen. Maybe you can get more for having an extra one."

The exchange completed, the storekeeper abruptly prepared for departure. "See you next week. Save your eggs."

Mahalie stood facing the rolling store, ignoring the dust it left hanging in the air around her. After it had gone about twenty yards, she heard the sound of a tap on the horn. She raised her empty hand to shoulder level, then jerked it back to her side.

Ottis could batter with the best of them. To deal with a minor infraction, say a cold biscuit or an irritating radio station, he would settle for a split lip produced by an almost casual backhand slap. When slapping, he preferred to use his right hand. Mahalie's lower lip split more often than her upper and, with accumulated scar tissue, became noticeably the thicker.

For a major offense, in particular any perceived reflection upon his failed performance as husband and provider, he favored his fists. In these instances, Ottis manifested his ambidexterity. A left cross or a jab with the right, either way he'd get his full weight behind it, aiming for the eyes where his mark of dominance would last for at least a week. It took him nearly two years to perfect these blows, striking so that the flesh of Mahalie's cheek was caught perfectly between his knuckles and her cheekbone, adding a grinding twist to maximize the internal tearing. The result was a permanent puff and shadow below eyes that became very adept at detecting the bunched muscles signaling an attack.

At first, Mahalie would heed her premonitions by ducking her head and raising her elbows. With time, and a couple of dislodged molars, she learned that obvious avoidance served only to further enrage Ottis. He'd storm her barricade, knock her elbows aside and straighten her with an uppercut. By their third anniversary, she'd perfected the technique of taking a half-step back the last moment before contact, thus lessening the impact. Ottis, drunk with the joy of causing hurt, never became aware of this maneuver.

For all the days of high summer, he came to her, pausing to tell her of a land of pearls and pomegranates, showing her the path to enlightenment and salvation.

Mahalie handed the storekeeper two dozen eggs. "Some's two or three days old."

"Don't matter. Town folks can't tell the difference. What d'you fancy, today?"

Mahalie looked around. Her eyes moved quickly over the Octagon soap and kitchen utensils. She spent some time with the rouge and mascara, then shook her head. "Maybe I'll get makeup next time." She tilted her head, looked past the storekeeper at the curtain. "You got anything really special?"

The storekeeper watched her eyes. "Back here." He reached behind himself and pushed aside the curtain.

"What's in there?"

He backed through the curtain and extended his hands to the left and right. "Take a look."

Mahalie followed him into the tiny room, looked around, and whispered, "Sweet Jesus." On one side, a damask-covered couch, barely wide enough for two, hugged the wall. Across from it crouched a low, black wooden table decorated with intricate carvings and inlays of mother of pearl. On the table was a small box of gleaming brass covered with engraving in an alphabet of curlicues. All around, on the floor and the walls and even the ceiling, were tapestries. Some featured flowers and unicorns. Tacked to the ceiling was a four by six galaxy of stars and planets in a violet infinity. Hanging behind the table was a depiction of men and women dressed in diaphanous gowns, cavorting in pools of blue and green water. All of this was illuminated by the dim light coming from a multicolored glass globe perched atop a tall, slim pedestal. "This where you live?"

The storekeeper laughed. "It's where I come alive." He draped himself over one end of the couch, his outstretched legs extended well under the table. "Have a seat."

Mahalie sat, her knees pressed together and her elbows tucked tightly into her ribs. She gestured with her chin toward the brass box. "What's in there?"

"Salvation."

Mahalie stood, bumping her head against several bamboo rods hanging from the ceiling and startling them into a four-note response. "Maybe that's funny in California but not around here."

The storekeeper remained sprawled on the couch. "No joke. It's my salvation from days of rolling the store and nights of thinking about rolling the store. Salvation from being in Nall County. Sit down. I'll introduce you to salvation."

Mahalie reclaimed her seat and watched while the storekeeper lifted the box, placed it on her lap, and opened it. Inside were thirty or more neat tubes of white paper, each maybe three inches long and no thicker than a pencil, their ends twisted tight. They looked like the roll-your-owns Ottis crafted with the rolling papers and drawstring sacks of Bull Durham he always bought before he bought groceries. "I don't smoke."

"Neither do I, not tobacco. These are special cigarettes, reefer, all the way from Siam." He reached into the box and touched the cigarettes. "Hand-rolled salvation." He removed five cigarettes from the box and handed four to Mahalie. "Two dozen worth. We'll share this one."

Mahalie mastered makeup. She discovered illusion and subtlety, learned that lipstick could imply a straighter lip and talcum would aid the pretense of a sweeter cheek. Even Ottis had grunted in surprise, if not appreciation. The storekeeper had been especially gallant this mellow late September morning, declaring that he could hardly see where she'd bumped into that door. Now settled into her corner of their secret room, she threw her head back and traveled among Mars and Saturn and Jupiter. "It makes the colors brighter, don't it?"

The storekeeper inhaled deeply, then held his breath while he passed the cigarette back to Mahalie. He held the smoke in until oxygen deprivation forced him to exhale and breathe. "The colors brighter and the mood lighter." He pointed at the reveling figures behind the table. "Watch 'em long enough and they'll start dancing."

Mahalie remained among the planets through in, hold, out. "You got to go to Siam to get more when this runs out?"

"No, no. My friend in San Francisco is the King of Cannabis. Imports it by the kilo. I've been wanting to get back to California, anyway."

"You leaving?"

"I've been offered a good price for the rolling store." He watched Mahalie struggle to keep her despair from showing, then smiled and laid a gentle hand on her forearm. "Not right away. Maybe in a few weeks." He glanced at the basket near her feet. "How many?"

Ottis shouted from the kitchen. "You gonna quit primping long enough to make breakfast?"

Mahalie replaced the cap on her Parisian Vermilion lipstick and picked up her hand-crafted tortoise shell comb. She made a couple of quick swipes through her scented hair, then laid the comb aside and headed for the kitchen. She crossed to the iron stove, plunged a fingertip into the cold grease coating the bottom of a frying pan, and began a pattern of curving lines. "There's not much except some leftover blackeyed peas."

"I'll not eat peas for breakfast. Make me some biscuits and fix me a plate of eggs. You got any more store-bought peaches?"

Abandoning her tracework, Mahalie took a baking soda can from the shelf behind the stove and ascertained that it was empty. "No biscuits. No more peaches. No more eggs."

Ottis shifted his weight so that he could look directly at her, causing the joints of his tattered cane chair to creak. "We been out of eggs for a month. Something getting in the hen house?"

"Fox, maybe."

"Mr. Fox also giving you all that makeup?"

Mahalie shrugged. "Maybe. You want the leftovers?"

Ottis stood, jabbing a finger toward Mahalie's face. "You want your lights knocked out?"

His spirit came to dwell within her, and she vowed to follow him.

The suitcase was small, but Mahalie had very little to pack. Her combs and pins, her jar of Turkish Beauty Balm, a couple of lipsticks, a tiny flask of Eau de Cologne, some face powder to cover the new bruise, her keepsake dimes. Atop these things, she placed a carefully folded cotton slip, pausing to touch its trim of delicate Belgian lace. She thought she had one remaining special cigarette, but a search turned up only a few brown flakes. "Never mind," she muttered. "There's more where that came from."

She looked around the bedroom, then took down a Baptist calendar Ottis had picked up somewhere. She kissed the picture of a young man with beautiful hair and urgent eyes, tore it from the calendar, placed it atop the slip, and threw the months on the floor. She closed the suitcase and bound it with a length of frayed clothesline. At the appointed time, Mahalie went to wait beside the road. She stood by the mailbox for maybe an hour, then sat in the weeds and rested her head on her suitcase.

Mahalie was still by the mailbox, fitfully asleep, when a scant afternoon rain came. Awakened, she tossed her head back and parted her lips. The raindrops washed the powder from her cheeks and the dryness from her throat. Her ablution complete, Mahalie remained beside the road, letting the sun dry her somewhat. About when the sun neared suppertime, she slapped the remaining droplets from her suitcase, tipped it onto its side, released its binding, and opened it. She removed the picture and sat looking at it. After awhile, she wadded the picture into a tight ball and tossed it into the ditch beside the road.

Fatback

Selma hated fatback. Hated its stubborn resistance to the cheap knife, the one Hulon said was good enough for her cooking. Hated its slimy persistence on her fingertips, long after it plopped into the frying pan. Hated the little brown spots on her hands, burns from hot grease ejected by the sizzling meat. Selma hated the ever-presence of fatback, a constant in days of dull labor followed by nights of restless regret.

At dawn, Selma had resented a mirror that reminded her how each day rendered her drier and more faded than was fair for a woman of twenty-four, a woman once called pretty. Now, her anger focused on her husband and fatback. Hulon required meat at every meal, which meant cooking, which meant adding to the heat in the kitchen. Even at mid-day, when most men would have settled for a spring-cooled glass of buttermilk and some cornbread left over from the previous day's supper, or a biscuit and fatback remaining from breakfast, Hulon expected her to coax new flame from the dormant embers in the iron stove and fry something. Even though he spent most mornings tending his still and sampling its product, he demanded to be fed as though he had toiled at honest work since daybreak. So, with noon approaching, the flat slap of the screen door announced that Selma Meacham was on her way, through the Alabama July dust and the cacophony of the dry flies, to get some fatback from the smokehouse.

The midday glare narrowed Selma's eyes to slits. She didn't see the intruder until she widened her eyes in the shade of the smokehouse porch. Finding herself facing him from no more than five feet, she abruptly halted and returned his stare. "Who're you?"

"I'm looking for work."

Selma studied his threadbare overalls, worn over a once-white shirt, and his sweat-stained fedora. She glanced at his shoes, covered with red dust, and knew he'd spent the morning walking. Most of all, she noted that his face had encountered no soap or razor for some time. Even poor field hands washed and shaved every day or so. Tramp, she decided.

"You think I got work in my smokehouse?" Selma knew that tramps would steal. Times were not as bad as before the war, but there were still those men who moved through the country, surviving by begging and stealing. A life that graced Selma with scant reward of her own produced in her little inclination toward charity or tolerance of misdemeanor.

"I didn't go in. I was just standing in this shade. I'll work for food."

"My husband didn't say nothing about needing help." Selma knew that Hulon's still was a solo operation. He preferred to retain a helper's share for his own consumption.

"Could I have a drink of water?"

Selma pointed with her chin toward the well.

"Thank you, ma'am."

While he drew some water, Selma moved farther into the shade. She watched while he poured an entire bucket of water into his gaunt frame. She surmised that, judging by the way his clothes hung from him, he normally carried at least fifty pounds more. Nobody ought to starve, she told herself, not even a tramp. Besides, if she gave him something to eat, he'd leave, most likely. "There's some old fatback you can have."

"Thank you, ma'am."

Selma nodded toward the tree-clad limestone ridge rising above the small pasture behind the smoke house. She took care

to indicate a direction opposite that of Hulon's still. "You can
take it with you and build yourself a little cook-fire up there,
in the woods. You got some matches?" Selma meant to ensure
that, once gone, he'd have no excuse to reappear. Having him
around when Hulon returned from distilling his morning run
of corn whiskey would lead, most likely, to some sort of ruckus.
She wanted none of that.

"Yes, ma'am."

"All right. Maybe you can pick a couple of apples on your
way. Wait here."

Selma stepped to the smokehouse door and removed the
wooden peg from the hasp, a security measure adequate for
keeping small animals from raiding the smokehouse but good
for little else. She'd told Hulon a lock would be better, but
he'd said they cost too much and a thief would just break it
open, anyway. She pushed the rough plank door open, stepped
through the portal, and paused to prepare for the ordeal. She
dreaded the crawl of spider webs across her bare arms, spiders
made all the more threatening by being unseen. She was
always repulsed by the thick odor of hickory-smoked meat, a
pungency she knew would stay in her nostrils long after she left
the smokehouse. Her eyes sought to give form to the shadows
among the hanging shapes. Near the door was the better meat,
hams and ribs that Hulon would exchange for sugar to supply
his still. Farther back, among terrifying shadows that shifted as
she approached, was the fatback, food for Hulon.

Selma waited until the shudder came and went, then
located the old piece of fatback she had decided the day before
was rancid enough to throw away. She lifted the slab of fatback
from its hook and turned to leave.

The tramp was standing in her path, his figure dark against
the brassy backlight of the sun and filling the doorway. He was
looking, not at Selma or at the hanging meat, but at the three
cardboard boxes in the nearest corner. Selma knew the boxes

contained jars of corn whiskey, hidden in the smokehouse where the sheriff might not think to look for them, waiting to be sold to the silent men who appeared in the yard almost every night. "I told you to wait outside."

"It's hot out there, so I came into the cool. What's in those boxes?"

"None of your business. Go back out."

He did not move. Fear charged through Selma. Alarm gripped her bowels. Her lungs strained for enough air to issue an outcry she knew no-one would hear. She denounced her foolish impulse toward charity. She knew better. She'd heard that some tramps did more than steal. Now, she was a woman alone, standing in a thin cotton dress, shivering on a hot day, trapped by a stranger in this airless place with disgusting and frightening things all around her.

"I didn't mean to scare you. I'll just take one of these. Your man won't miss a little one." He took a pint jar from one of the boxes and slipped it into a side pocket, creating a noticeable bulge. He hesitated for a moment, then stepped back through the door and to one side, removing his hat and exposing a head of thinning, silver, recently combed hair. Bowing slightly, he swept her way clear with his hat.

Selma rushed from the smokehouse, taking care to stand between the tramp and the house. "Here. You can have all of it, but you better go."

"Thank you, ma'am." He tucked the meat under his arm, replaced his hat on his head, and strode away, moving faster than Selma had expected. Turning to enter the house, Selma understood the tramp's haste. Hulon was approaching from the other side of the well. Selma noted that he looked rather like the tramp. Her husband was heavier and younger and somewhat cleaner, but dressed in the same country style of overalls and old hat and heavy shoes.

"Who was that?"

"Tramp, I guess."

"What was you doing in the smokehouse with him?"

"Getting him some old fatback, and he came in out of the heat. He didn't take nothing, except what I gave him."

"He get into my whiskey?"

"No." Selma turned and walked toward the house.

Hulon followed her. "Fatback's all you gave him? What was in his pocket?"

"I told him he could pick some apples. Maybe he already did."

"Dinner done?"

Selma didn't answer. She'd forgotten her original purpose. Now, she'd have to listen to him fuss about waiting to eat. She stopped, turned, and went back to the smokehouse.

The autumn chill had silenced the dry flies but had not advanced to the point of driving Hulon indoors. He assumed his accustomed afternoon position on the front porch, sitting in his decrepit rocking chair, a quart jar of corn whiskey on the floor beside him, his Model 1903 Springfield rifle across his knees, sipping from the jar and waiting for something to kill. Hulon had avoided the draft until 1944 but the sheriff had finally taken him in and the military police had been waiting. After three months and four psychological evaluations, the army had wisely decided that Hulon had it right, in the first place. He and the army were totally unsuited for each other, he'd never make a soldier. On his way home, he managed to steal the already-outdated rifle from the training battalion armory. The trophy became his constant and, except for a jar of whiskey, only companion on the porch, its .30 caliber bullets reducing most birds to a puff of feathers. Hulon did not hunt, he killed. The ripped carcasses lay where they fell until they became a part of the soil. Now, many of the birds had already gone farther South and there were fewer targets. Still, he waited for something to present itself for killing.

Hulon looked at Selma when she emerged from the interior of the house, on her way to the mailbox. "Can't hide that anymore, can you?"

"What?"

He gestured toward her belly. "I can count jars and I can count months. You and that tramp was drinking my whiskey and messing around."

"Don't be a fool, Hulon. I got no interest in your whiskey or in messing around with some tramp." She rubbed her swollen belly. "You planted this seed." Their rare coupling had taken Selma by surprise. Hulon usually took what was left of his sodden ardor elsewhere. Selma remembered the sudden attack, stumbling backwards and falling, trying to rise but being crushed against the bare wood floor by a body stinking of whiskey and sweat and lust. She remembered the pain of his thrust and brief pumping. She remembered the humiliation of being left, soiled, on the floor while he went in search of another jar.

"That army doctor said I can't make children."

"That was four years ago and he told you it was temporary. Some kind of infection. Didn't that medicine clear it up?"

Hulon took a sip. "Don't know. Never saw that doctor again."

"Because they ran you off." Selma stepped off the porch, paused, presented her body's profile to Hulon. "But, if it's tall and skinny, we ought to call it Smoky."

Hulon squinted at Selma's stiff back as she marched toward the mailbox. Glancing away from her, he detected some movement at the edge of the yard and aimed his rifle toward a partially-denuded white oak tree. Then, he swung the Springfield down and to the left, jerking the trigger with enough force to spoil his aim. The heavy bullet took Selma high in her right shoulder, causing her to stumble forward, then pitch head-long into the path. Seeing that she was attempting to rise, Hulon chambered another round and fired again. The second bullet ripped a red gash along Selma's left side, spraying blood onto the weeds. She collapsed and remained motionless. Hulon lifted the jar of corn whiskey from the floor, held it at eye level so he could check the quantity of its contents, then took a sip.

Selma was still sprawled in the yard when the mailman came. "Mr. Meacham? What's happened here?"

Hulon stood, rifle in one hand and jar in the other, and entered the house. The mailman, his mind crowded with images of a downed woman and a bolt-action rifle, hesitated. Seeing no movement in the house, he went to Selma, picked her up, and carried her to his car. He drove away with as much speed as a pre-war Hudson would allow, hunched over the steering wheel in an effort to present less of a target. He fully expected a bullet in the back of his head, but none came.

At the Nall County Medical Clinic, the postman screeched to a stop and bolted from his sedan, leaving the door open and the motor running. He grabbed an orderly by the elbow and half coaxed, half dragged him out to the car. They both halted at the sight of Selma leaning against the rear fender of the Hudson.

Selma returned their stares for a moment, then demanded through teeth clenched with pain, "Y'all gonna help me or let me bleed to death?"

The sheriff stopped in the side yard, near the house and in sight of the smokehouse. He told his deputy to stay in the car, then got out and stood behind the open car door. "Mr.

Meacham, you at home?" He always cautioned his deputies to be especially cautious with domestic disputes. The anger was too easily redirected toward anyone foolish enough to intercede. "Hulon?"

The shot came from the smokehouse door. It shattered the windshield of the Plymouth, sending the deputy diving toward the floorboard and confirming the sheriff's opinion of these situations. The sheriff drew his pistol but did not fire. Instead, he crouched behind the car door, peering cautiously around the edge. "This ain't necessary, Hulon. Selma's alive. Put that ought-three down and come on out of there."

The sheriff saw the movement of a rifle barrel through the partially open door of the smokehouse and jerked his head back. The second shot kicked up dirt near his feet. "Clyde. Take the shotgun. Ease around to the other side of the house and get yourself a good position. He's forted up in the smokehouse. My guess is, that's where he keeps his whiskey, which means he's drunk. Just keep him boxed up while I go get some help."

"Yes, sir." Clyde opened the passenger door and dashed to the cover of the house. While the sheriff was backing out of the yard, Clyde circled around to the well. He positioned himself with his shotgun pointed over the rock rim of the well, toward the smokehouse. He waited a couple of minutes, then muttered to himself, "Might've got out while I was coming around the house." He stood, taking care to keep his shotgun pointed toward the smokehouse. "Mr. Meacham?" Receiving no word or shot in reply, Clyde began moving cautiously away from the well.

The sheriff had seen the smoke from a mile away. By the time he drove into the yard, the roof of the smokehouse was fully ablaze. Clyde was lying face down on top of his shotgun, near the well. The sheriff knelt beside him and spoke softly. "Damn, boy. I told you to just stay put." Then, he rose and spoke to the nearest deputy. "Billy, take care of Clyde."

Billy approached Clyde's body, stopped and stared. "Head's blowed almost clean off."

"That's what an ought-three does to you. Put him in my car. Put that old quilt down, first. It's in the trunk. Al, take Price and check the house and the barn. Don't take any chances. I got enough dead deputies." The sheriff stood, watching the fire while his orders were carried out.

Their tasks completed, the three deputies began drawing water from the well. Al reported to the sheriff. "He ain't around here. You think he's down at his still, or what?"

The sheriff nodded toward the smokehouse. "I reckon he's in there."

"Burned himself up? Damn."

"Hard to say. Clyde's shotgun's been fired, maybe that set it off. I'll say this. Hulon was not one to put himself in the chair and he'd killed a deputy." No-one mentioned Selma.

Billy chuckled. "Smells like barbecue, don't it?"

"Hush up your foolishness." The sheriff pointed toward the smokehouse. "Y'all quit drinking that water and get to throwing it on the fire."

The deputies retrieved a water bucket from the house and went to work. Before they had passed half a dozen buckets-full, there was a muffled explosion within the smokehouse, blowing the door outward. The rush of flame nearly engulfed Price.

"You okay?"

Price gingerly touched his face, then looked at his hands. "Got singed but I'm okay, I guess. That must've been his whiskey."

Because there was only one bucket, the deputies had little impact on the fire. In well less than an hour, the smokehouse was reduced to a pile of embers and bones.

The Righteous Hammer of Jehovah

Grady cursed the barbed wire and imagined Miss Meadows coming to him along the fenceline. She'd take his hand in hers, look with concern at his ripped palm, comfort him with soothing words. She'd exaggerate the pain, tell him he was brave. He'd say it don't hurt that bad.

While the blood dried in the crease of his wound he wiped sweat from his eyes and squinted into the summer glare. The crop threatened failure, brown edges on curling green leaves, stunted and uncertain in the cracked soil. Across the field of corn the woods stood in a haze of heat and dust and distance. If Grady put down his hammer and made his way between the rows, reached the stand of live oaks, it would be cooler there. Repairs were useless. Mr. Busby's cows would again brave the barbs separating their seared pasture from the corn. They'd strain through to the somewhat greener forage and pull the rusting wire loose from the cedar posts. His father would send him again to sweat and blister and long for relief among the live oaks.

Grady tested his injured grip on the hammer, grimaced, returned to his task. He assuaged his pain with the memory of Miss Meadows standing before her class, reading poetry that went beyond *Casey at the Bat*, poetry abut colors and light and love. She'd chastised the class, most of them, for looking sideways at each other and giggling. She'd looked to the back of the room and her eyes had touched those of the tall, thin boy who'd been kept back twice for missing months of school at a time. Grady was grateful for this private inclusion, this reaching beyond the circle of younger boys and girls who invited each other to birthday parties where their parents surprised them with radios. Buster Browns, he called them. Miss Meadows knew, he was sure, that he grasped the full meaning when she spoke of hearts that beat in unison, that he was not dreaming of old baseball games or new hair bobs. He pounded the staples into the sun-hardened cedar, knew that blood from his wound was soaking into the wooden handle of the hammer and did not care. He imagined Miss Meadows among the live oaks, sitting on a quilt with Tabby curled up beside her. Sitting barefoot on a red and blue Fleur-de-Lis with her skirt above her knees.

Woodrow Cox claimed to farm his forty acres but mainly he hawked the holy word for tightly folded dollars scented by the folds of flesh where they'd been secreted. He was an itinerant peddler for Chicago Holiness Publishing and his territory was all of Alabama. When Grady was younger, he traveled with his father from one clap-board country chapel to another. The resident preacher, for a share of the take, would invite Woodrow into the pulpit.

Woodrow, his balding head bejeweled with sweat, would strut and shudder and shout out images of the hell-fire awaiting all transgressors. His particular talent lay in denouncing fornicators. At the climax of his rant, he'd extend a quivering hand toward the congregation—the strong right hand of Almighty Jehovah he called it. He'd detect the presence, right there in the sanctuary, of unrepentant Eves who used their charms to lure the lust of Adam within men. He'd declare, his voice rising to a high pitch of passion, that he could feel their hearts throbbing against his fingertips, could smell the stench of unholy copulation that lingered about their bodies. He'd have half the women red-faced and squirming while the other half glared accusingly at them and at the grinning menfolk.

Woodrow always concluded with the stern assurance that the congregation's best hope of staving off ol' Beelzebub lay in the regular reading of the tracts he sold from an ancient leather valise. Two dollars for the plain version, four dollars for the illustrated edition. The higher priced booklets sold well because they had pictures of little red devils engaged in the carnal acts he'd spoken of, helpful so folks would know exactly what to watch out for.

Sometimes, a sister of the congregation would invite them to stay over. Grady would sleep on a pallet on the parlor floor while his father acquainted the good woman with the twists and tares on the path to righteousness. The year he turned twelve, Grady asked his father if the nocturnal thumps and yowls were the sounds of sin being purged. Thereafter, he was left on the farm to plow and plant. By sixteen he was the farmer of the family, with his father performing occasional roles of supervisor and inspector. Grady went to school whenever he could.

The last week of August, Woodrow called Grady in from pulling weeds in the kitchen garden. "I've been called to do the Lord's work down in the Wiregrass. You'll stay home this fall and work this farm. You've been exposed to enough of your Miss Meadows and her poems."

"Miss Meadows goes to church. New Hope Missionary Baptist."

"Church doors are open to saints and sinners, alike." Woodrow plunged a hand into the bib pocket of his overalls and withdrew his annotated pulpit copy of *By Faith Alone Shall Ye Know*. He paged through until he found an underlined passage, then held it a few inches from his son's face. "Read what it says. Right there." Woodrow jabbed at the page with a rigid finger. "Revealed and uninterpreted." He paused, drew in some mind-clearing oxygen, exhaled. "Ain't no need for any readin' except the divinely revealed word of God, no need for heathen poetry favored by female school teachers." When his son failed to take the little book from his hand he returned it to its carrying place, securing it with a pat. "The word of God. That's all you need."

Grady took a step back. "I'll get two weeks off from school at cotton-picking time and that's enough for what little cotton and corn we'll get."

Woodrow responded to his son's counterproposal by dropping to his knees. "Kneel, boy. We'll pray on this."

Grady did as he was told. He half-listened to his father's plea for God to show his son the true way. When Woodrow nodded to him Grady launched into the sort of double prayer he'd perfected during many hours on his knees. Aloud, he begged Our Heavenly Father to forgive him for wanting to be in school instead of in the fields. Silently, he beseeched Sweet Jesus to clear his way back to Miss Meadows. He ended with a solemn Amen and waited for his earthly father to render final judgment.

Woodrow struggled to his feet. "Well, at least you begged for forgiveness. Brother Josephus says in *On Your Knees* that's the first step. I reckon I'll settle for that but you better get your work done, too."

Grady offered up a second Amen.

School was declared back in session the day after Labor Day. Grady overheard the excited titter among the girls before he saw the glitter on Miss Meadows' left hand. A pilot, said the class know-it-all, handsome as the day is long, from up North. Got lost here in Nall County trying to find a short cut to Memphis. Stopped in Ebenezer and went into the drug store for a cold drink and some directions. Just by blind luck, Miss Meadows was sitting at the counter having a dish of vanilla ice cream.

One thing led to another. The pilot ended up hanging around for a week. Swept Miss Meadows off her feet, if you know what I mean. He's in England now but he'll be back and they'll get married. Grady mumbled a greeting to Miss Meadows, headed for the back row, slouched in the last desk in the corner.

Throughout September, Grady waited for Miss Meadows to lock her gray eyes on his and reveal the feelings behind words, emotions that none other would understand. He watched her stroll back and forth, offer a sonnet for all to consider, invite her students to savor the rhythm of the words. She cast her voice about the room, but never to him alone.

The last day of September, Miss Meadows was absent. The principal explained that they'd have a substitute for the rest of the week while Miss Meadows recovered from some bad news. In the fall of 1942 everyone knew what that meant. A knocked-on door would be opened, a nervous man in a dress uniform would deliver a rehearsed speech and, the next day, a gold star would appear in a front room window. There were stories that in some places boys would throw rocks at official-looking cars, try to drive them and their message away.

Miss Meadows returned the next Monday. She mentioned her fiancé just once, said there's always hope and someone reported seeing a parachute. Grady felt his heart pressing against his ribs. He forgave her for ignoring him, understood it was her patriotic duty to think only of her brave pilot. He imagined her forehead lightly on his shoulder, dignified tears barely wetting her cheeks. He'd tell her it was God's will and kiss her tears away.

Autumn brought news of Guadalcanal. A procession of Marines marched across the front page, grinning privates with their caps cocked defiantly to one side and hard-eyed sergeants who'd killed dozens of fanatical Japs. In the face of such competition Miss Meadows' pilot was diminished as a subject of popular speculation. Grady hated his growing conviction that someone, he, must demonstrate unflagging admiration for her courage and strength. He dreaded the risk, feared he'd never reclaim the safety of unspoken longing, worried that she'd see his concern for what it was and reject it.

His strategy was to lift her spirits by rendering little helps. At the bell, when others rushed from the room, he paused to straighten a book knocked askew on its shelf or drop an abandoned paper wad into the wastebasket. After a week of this, just when he was beginning to think it fruitless, Miss Meadows rewarded him with a slight smile and a nod. It was the first exclusive acknowledgment she'd offered him that school year.

The following week Grady spent a full two minutes in departing, went along the wall of windows and returned each windowshade to a neat half-mast position. On Tuesday Miss Meadows said that looked much better. On Wednesday, she adjusted one shade herself while he attended to the other four.

On Thursday Miss Meadows pointed at a box of books by her desk. "Grady, would you carry those to my car, please?" Her fiancé had left his car in her care, a car suited in spirit and grace to Miss Meadows, a 1941 Chrysler Windsor convertible, the only one of its kind in Nall County. Grady closed the trunk lid and turned to go but Miss Meadows' voice stopped him. "It's a warm day for October. Help me put the top down and I'll give you a ride home."

Grady's throat closed and he could only nod. The top stowed, he sat beside Miss Meadows, straight and still, praying that she'd drive slowly and all the young and bright and clean would see them. Miss Meadows did not drive slowly, did not conserve her rationed gasoline. Instead, she gunned the engine as soon as they were away from the school and Grady had managed to explain where he lived. From the corner of his eye he watched her tilt her head back and shake her brown hair loose, watched her wet her lips with the tip of her tongue.

"So, tell me about your family."

"There's just me and pa. Ma's dead."

"How sad, to lose your mother."

"Pa said she ran off to live in sin. I reckon she's dead because I never heard from her."

Miss Meadows glanced at her passenger. "Grady, please let me apologize for asking such personal questions." Neither spoke for awhile.

"So, what will you do when you finish school?"

Grady shrugged. "Don't know. Maybe join the navy. Or the air corps." He felt a rush of self-loathing. That was stupid, he told himself, mentioning the service that took her pilot. Miss Meadows lapsed back into quiet while Grady silently prayed that the God of Mercy would cause the awkwardness to pass.

Not one classmate saw his moment of glory but his father was at the mailbox when they arrived at the turnoff. Woodrow approached the car and stared across his son at Miss Meadows.

Miss Meadows smiled. "Good afternoon. You must be Mr. Cox. I'm Catherine Meadows, Grady's English teacher."

Woodrow peered at this woman with tumbled hair and color in her cheeks. He touched the brim of his misshapen hat with two fingers of his right hand.

Miss Meadows nodded in return. "Grady's a good student. He has a very mature understanding of literature. And he's been very helpful to me."

Woodrow's lanky knees jerked within his overalls. His feet shuffled in the red dirt. His eyes took on an unwavering set and a hard brightness came into them. He took a quick breath through his mouth, clamped his jaws shut. He took a step closer to the car.

Grady knew what he was seeing. The spirit had come into his father, had alerted him to the presence of a temptress. A righteous wrath was coming to a boil within Woodrow Cox and would soon come spewing out of his mouth. "Pa."

Woodrow ignored the warning word. He unclenched his jaws. "Well, Cathy Meadows, now I see why Grady likes school so much." A grin peeled thin lips back from stained teeth. "Can't say as I blame him." His nostrils flared a bit, tested the heated air for the scent of her.

Grady got out of the pilot's beautiful red convertible and stood between his father and the pilot's beautiful fiancée. Miss Meadows drove away, waving but not looking back. Grady attempted to walk around his father but was stopped by a hand clutching his shoulder.

"Boy, she might think you're mature, but you got your sights set way too high."

Grady pulled away, left his father with his right hand raised.

Woodrow turned his hand into a fist with one protruding finger. "They say when that yankee tomcat came sniffing around she let him have everything he wanted." He nodded. "Now he's gone and got hisself shot down and you're studying on taking his place."

Grady raised an open palm against his father's accusation. "You don't know nothing about that."

Woodrow's narrowed eyes searched his son's face for evidence of continuing rebellion. When Grady lowered his hand Woodrow did the same. "Soon's we get to the house you're going to read *The Wiles of Jezebel and Her Sisters*. All the way through. You still got a lot to learn about the female creature." He took the time to hawk and spit. "And you never did know what to do about stray cats. Your remember that?"

Grady remembered. He remembered the day he turned ten. He remembered how he'd yearned for a Winchester lever-action, the cowboy kind. Other boys his age already had a .22 and his father had said he'd think about it. Even a bolt-action

Remington, a single-shot, would do. Red Ryder BB guns were for little kids. A .22 was a grown-up gun. Today was the day, sure as shootin'. When his father told him to quit chopping cotton and come to the barn, he had mischief dancing across his face and he kept waving, come on, hurry up. Probably has it hid right there where he's pointing, Grady thought.

Woodrow was bent over a pile of feed sacks. "Look what I found."

Grady closed his eyes and whispered to God and Jesus and all the angels in heaven that he'd be good forever if it was a Winchester. Then he opened his eyes and looked behind the feed sacks into the worried eyes of a yellow and white cat, lying on her side and nursing five kittens. Three of the babies were near copies of their mother but two had inherited splotches of black from their sire.

Woodrow nudged his son with an elbow. "Your stray cat has multiplied."

Grady stared at the feline family. He'd seen birth before, piglets and a spindly-legged calf, but these were his first kittens.

"Them kittens got to go."

Grady struggled to shift from the disappointment of no rifle to understanding what his father had in mind. "We going to give 'em away?"

Woodrow picked up an empty feed sack and handed it to his son. "We'll give 'em to Mr. Rivers." He chuckled. "Yeah, Mr. Rivers. Sack 'em up." He left the barn.

The mother cat paced, anxiety written on her face. Her eyes followed Grady's hand as he lifted her newborn, one by one, and gently placed them in the burlap bag. After the last kitten disappeared into the sack, Grady extended a reassuring hand toward their mother, but she shied away from him and tried to peer into the bag. He stood, gathered the top of the bag, carefully lifted the squirming burden. "We can't have this many cats, Tabby. Mr. Rivers'll take care of 'em." He turned away from Tabby.

Woodrow stood in the door. "Put mamma cat in there, too."

"I thought you said just the kittens."

Woodrow returned to the shadows of the barn. "Changed my mind. Babies need their mamma to nurse, don't they?" For several minutes, he watched his son's half-hearted efforts to catch the now thoroughly alarmed cat. Then, he joined in the chase and together they cornered Tabby. Woodrow managed to avoid her slashing claws and gripped the loose skin at the back of her neck. He lifted the frantic, screeching feline and dropped her into the maw of the sack as soon as Grady opened it. "Tie it off or she'll get out. That's one mad cat."

Grady said he needed to get back to work but his father insisted that he come along. "You can say your last good-byes. Put 'em in the truck. In the back."

The cats remained still and quiet until the truck began to move. Then Tabby began to struggle against the unyielding burlap, adding her energy to the movement of the bag on the bouncing truck bed. She set up a guttural cry of frustration and despair, counterpointed by the mewling of the infants but nearly drowned out by the rattle and roar of the decrepit, unmuffled pickup.

With his son sitting stiffly beside him, Woodrow took the unpaved road that connected their parcel of red dirt to the rest of Nall County. They drove past Mr. Busby's extensive holdings and into an area of cut-over pine forest. Evergreens of adequate girth for pulping had been stripped from the land, leaving an ugly tangle of trimmings, pushed-over lesser trees, and scraggly third growth struggling up through the deadwood to reach the light. On the far side of the logged-out expanse was a creek crossed by a one-lane wooden bridge. Woodrow stopped halfway across the bridge, switched off the motor and set the handbrake. "Here we are. Mr. Rivers. Get your cats."

The only sound other than the rasp of the cicadas in the willows along the creek bank was the hoarse caterwaul of the doomed cats. Grady remained in place, look out and down at the muddy water creeping along under the bridge, tried not to know what his father had in mind. He'd overheard some boys in school talking about this preferred method for disposing of surplus cats. But until now he'd not made the connection. "They'll all drown."

Woodrow barked a single peal of laughter. "That's the idea, boy."

"I can't do it."

Woodrow reached across Grady and unlatched the passenger-side door. "You took in a stray cat. You let her out when she was in heat. Now, you're the one to get rid of 'em."

Grady got out of the truck, lifted the bundle from the bed, stood by the bridge railing. The stream was partially clogged with silt, run-off from the denuded land nearby, but the middle of the creek looked deep enough for his father's purpose. He turned to his father. "Can't we do something beside drowning 'em?"

Woodrow emitted another guffaw. "Boy, you're something. Tell you what. Get the hammer and bust their skulls. That'll be faster." Seeing that his son remained immobile, Woodrow snorted in exasperation, rummaged through the toolbox until he found the claw hammer, snatched the laden gunny sack from Grady's hand. He dropped the bag beside the rear wheel of the truck, knelt, pounded the bag until it was silent and unmoving. He stood and turned to his son. "I did the killing for you. At least, you can throw 'em in."

The natural color had drained from Grady's face. For a moment, he remained silent and unmoving, transfixed by the death scene. Then he grasped the knotted top of the bag and lifted it. He shook it but there was no response. He extended the bag over the rail and released it. Tabby and her family splashed into the dirty water beneath his feet. Because his father had overlooked the important precaution of weighting the sack of cats with a rock, they did not immediately sink. Grady watched the bag move with the turgid current until enough water seeped through the rough weave of the burlap shroud and it sank from sight.

School went on and October went on, most days still sunny but cooler than the one before. On the last Friday of that month of change, after the shades were attended to, Miss Meadows stood close to Grady. He inhaled the scent of her, of soap and starch and the warm milk smell of her breath. He felt a quickening in his loins. She gently touched the underside of his wrist. "Please come to my house and help me move some furniture. I'll make cocoa."

This time his voice did not fail him. "I'd be glad to." A step before they reached her car Grady leapt ahead, opened the driver's door with his left hand, placed his right forearm across his waist, bowed. "Your carriage, ma'am."

Miss Meadows laughed, curtsied, took her place behind the wheel. Then she got out. "Can you drive a car?"

"I've been driving my pa's pickup since I was twelve." When Miss Meadows waved him into the driver's seat he did not hesitate. He started the Chrysler into life, marveled at its quiet engine and smooth clutch. He eased away from the curb, afraid to breathe because even a small change in the equilibrium of the mood might shatter it. He barely heard Miss Meadows' directions to her house but he'd long since scouted out the place where she lived. He drove as slowly as he dared and this time they were there, a dozen or more Buster Browns walking home from school. All gaped, a few grinned, one waved. Grady felt compelled to ignore the wave but was grateful to Miss Meadows for returning it. Even better that she should blithely signal her awareness that they'd been seen together and he was driving her car.

Grady eased the Chrysler around a corner onto Miss Meadows' street. He turned toward her and asked if he should park at the curb or in her driveway. Instead of answering she caught her breath and leaned slightly forward, suddenly pale and looking through the windshield at the olive drab sedan parked in front of her house. Grady parked the convertible behind the army vehicle and sat, not speaking and not moving.

Miss Meadows was half-way to the house when he came out onto the porch. She stopped, screamed, fell to the ground. Her pilot, whole and strong and resplendent in his ribbons and wings and bars, came to her, lifted her, held her, took her inside. Neither of them looked back at the convertible or the teenage boy walking away from it.

In November of 1942 recruiters did not waste time on proof of birthdate. If a likely-looking youth claimed to be of age he was rushed through a physical and told to raise his right hand. Grady asked to become a pilot but was told the most a high school dropout could expect was gunner's school. He went home and told his father he intended to join the air corps.

Woodrow was seated at the kitchen table, making notes from *Wrath of Jehovah* in preparation for his next sojourn. "You think wearing the same uniform will win her back?" He closed the pamphlet and began tapping it on the table. "A true believer would call God's wrath down on him. She can't help herself, she's weak like all females. It's him what needs to be dealt with." He extended the pamphlet toward his son. "'Strike from your midst he that would lure your women into lust.' Says that, right here."

Grady snatched *Jehovah* from Woodrow's hand and hurled it across the room. "Nothing in your books has got anything to do with this."

For a long moment Woodrow watched his son try to blink away the tears threatening to spill down his cheeks. "You never did have the gumption to do what needed doin'." He retrieved his text from the floor.

Grady was in his second week of boot camp when they came for him, an MP and two sheriff's deputies. The MP cuffed him but surrendered him to the civilian authorities because, although his alleged felony was against a military officer, it took place before his actual enlistment. The deputies drove all night to get back to Nall County where they locked Grady in a bare cell with no bed. After a few hours sleep for themselves and none for Grady they escorted their prisoner into a room with a table and some chairs and began their questioning. Grady, conditioned by the repetitive harangue of Woodrow's prayers and preachments, hunkered down within himself and endured four hours of interrogation. When the deputies left the room one slapped the back of Grady's head.

Ten minutes later Grady was joined by a deputy with a fresh shave and a pressed uniform, a man about six years older than he. "Afternoon, Grady." The deputy did not wait for a reply. "I'm Deputy Busby. My daddy's got the place next to yours." Deputy Busby sat down and placed a tall bottle of Royal Crown Cola on the table separating him from Grady. "Here's a cold drink for you. Now listen to me. I went through law enforcement training down in Tuscaloosa last year. I learned a lot about crime detection. Motive. Opportunity. Means. Ever heard of that?" Again the deputy did not wait for a reply. "First, motive. Several kids at the high school told us about how Miss Meadows encouraged your crush on her, lettin' you drive her car and all." The deputy chuckled. "Can't say I blame you. That's one fine looking woman."

He waited while Grady took a long drink of RC. "Opportunity took awhile. Finally old lady Banks came forward with a recollection. Somebody wearing overalls and skinny like you, with an old hat pulled down to hide his face, was hanging around Miss Meadows' house. It was the day Miss Meadows came home from school and found her yankee pilot with his head stove in." Deputy Busby leaned toward Grady. "The same day the recruiter swore you in and sent you off to boot camp."

"Last, means. All your daddy wanted to do was whoop and holler about righteous vengeance and stray cats. Sounds a little tetched in the head if you don't mind me saying so. He wouldn't let us on his property so we got a search warrant. The hammer had been throwed up into the hay loft. The lab found blood on the head and more blood on the handle. We got medical records from the military for you and for that pilot. Guess what." The deputy slid the half-empty RC across the table until it was beyond Grady's reach. "It was that pilot's blood on the head and your blood on the handle."

Deputy Busby removed a folded sheet of paper from his shirt pocket. "It all adds up, Grady." He unfolded the typewritten page and placed it before Grady. "We've got the evidence to convict you, but that's not the reason for you to sign this statement. The main reason is, she'll be there and she'll hear it all." The deputy paused, allowed Grady to imagine the courtroom scene, his father calling down judgment on all fornicators and poets, the prosecutor waving the bloody hammer, Miss Meadows sobbing. "She's been through enough, Grady. End it if you really do care about her. Do the right thing."

VJ Day, victory over Japan, was announced over the intercom. It was over. The heroes would come home, the future was brighter than it had been in a generation. Grady stood by the cedar post and looked through the barbed wire. It was the best field of corn he'd ever seen, dark green, tall, rustling in the warm breeze, smelling of damp soil, full of life. Someday maybe they'd send him through the gates with the other convicts to make a crop of corn. But for now he could only work inside the compound. He pulled the wire taut, took care to avoid the barbs. He swung the hammer, pounded the staples into the sun-hardened wood.

Strip Pit

"You want it all?" Janelle watched a grin grow on the large, square face of the man standing at her teller station.

Sonny nodded. "Yeah, darlin'. I want it all." He stared at the nametag pinned above her left breast. "Janelle."

Janelle managed to keep her color down. She studied her computer screen and her eyes widened. "It's been accumulating interest for thirty years."

"My momma put money in here on my first birthday. How much is it?"

"One thousand, four hundred and twenty-eight dollars. And seventy-five cents. How do you want it?"

Sonny's grin broadened. "Any way I can get it."

Janelle lost control of her color and her patience. "What I mean is, cash or check?"

"Cash. I'm gonna get me a car. Might come back and take you for a ride."

Janelle did not respond, except to count out Sonny's withdrawal.

The high summer sun nearly succeeded in defeating the air-conditioning of Ebenezer First Methodist Church. In a back pew, Clarence Loomis sat next to his daughter and mouthed the words of a hymn. *In seasons of distress and grief.* Clarence closed his hymnal and looked up, at the stained glass window behind the pulpit, at the glowing face of Jesus. *And oft escaped the tempter's snare.* He glanced sideways at the fidgeting teenager.

After the service, Frances waited by their Buick while Clarence went among the five generations of Methodists at eternal rest beside the church. He stopped at a grave with a large headstone of bright marble and stood with his hands joined in front of him. He told his wife their daughter might pass summer school, and he was doing the best he could to raise her. He stood in silence for a minute, nodded, then promised to get Frances to church more often.

Clarence rounded the corner of the church, then began to walk faster when he saw two young men standing close to his daughter. One, the smaller of the two, scurried away as soon as he saw Clarence approaching. The other made an attempt at returning Clarence's glare, then shrugged and turned away to join his companion. Clarence pointed toward the passenger side door. "In the car, Miss."

"We was just talking." Frances did as she was ordered, but slammed the door with enough force to make her father wince.

"Damn. Floyd never said nothing about you being a big ol' red-headed white boy."

Sonny sized up the man he had just driven seventy miles to see. Staring back at him was a slender, close-cropped black man about his age, with a trace of mirth chasing surprise across his face. Sonny ran his left hand through his hair. "I guess I could dye it." He lowered his hand and swiped it across the front of his tee shirt, wiping away the sweat and dust his fingers had combed from his hair. He placed his hand on his cheek and grinned. "Hard to stop being white, though."

Dewey chuckled and opened the screen door. "Come on in. That Floyd always was a jokester. How'd you come to be buds with him down there in Ashwater?"

Sonny stepped through the door of the small, porchless frame house. Although the windows were open, the still day had produced no breeze to stir the heat packed into the small rooms. "After I did my turn on the chain gang, they put me in the woodwork shop. Floyd showed me how to operate the machines and I helped him draw some designs for the warden's lawn furniture. After that, we worked together. "

"Ain't that opposite what the Nation of Islam and them Aryan Nation peckerwoods believe in?"

Sonny followed Dewey across the front room, toward the kitchen. "In the yard, he hung with his people. I stayed with mine. When there was a hassle, we both just backed away from it."

"Good for y'all." Dewey snatched a dozen fast food containers off the kitchen table and pitched them into a sink full of dirty dishes. "Cold one?"

"Damn straight. Thanks." Sonny accepted the bottle of malt liquor, twisted off the cap, sat down, and lifted the bottle to his host. "I appreciate you helping me get a job."

"What I told Floyd was, I'd try."

"Trying is all I'm asking. What's the job?"

"Coal. Strip mining."

"I passed some pits on my way up here. Ugly."

Dewey nodded. "Nowadays, the government makes the company back-fill. With the older ones, the rain filled 'em up and it's like there's no bottom. No telling what's down in there. Anyway, it's about the only work around here. It's either strip mine, get on the dole, or rob folks. Take your pick."

"I don't beg and I'm done with robbing. I'll work. What'll I be doing?"

"Blasting crew, most likely. Cast blasting." Dewey put his bottle down and, with his cigarette leaving smoke trails in the air, made lift-and-throw motions with his hands. "We drill a hole, then drop some ANFO in with the primer and a cap. The blaster wires it for the shot."

"What's ANFO?"

"Ammonium nitrate and fuel oil, what amounts to fertilizer mixed with diesel fuel." Dewey paused to take a drink. "You afraid of getting blowed up?"

Sonny shrugged. "More afraid of being broke. I'm wondering how I'm gonna support myself until my first paycheck."

"You can stay here for a while. I'll stake you to a few cheeseburgers."

Sonny nodded. "Floyd said you'd be decent." He swallowed half of his malt liquor. "Any action around here?"

"Action? Like, women?"

"What else?"

Dewey sat his bottle down and directed a narrow-eyed stare at Sonny. "You one of them white guys, think you'll change your luck with a black girl?"

Sonny raised his palms toward Dewey. "I ain't saying nothing like that. I just figured you know your way around, is all."

Dewey studied the label on his malt liquor bottle. "You'd be better off looking around Birmingham. More to choose from."

Sonny twisted one corner of his mouth upward. "I tried to get something going down there with this bank teller. Janelle, cute little thing. But it didn't work out."

"Well, there's not much action hereabouts, black or white. The preachers keep most of the married women on the straight and narrow. The single ones head for Birmingham or Memphis soon as they can. There's the high school stuff, but you look a little old for that."

Sonny lifted both hands and back-stroked the sweaty hair at his temples. "I may be thirty-one, but I can still rock and roll."

Dewey lit another Kool. "There's this one white chick, Frances Loomis, comes around the pit sometimes. Her daddy's the certified blaster. He's my boss, might be yours. She likes to seine around the men when her daddy's looking the other way."

Sonny placed his forearms on the table. "What you figure she's seining for?"

Dewey took a long drag on his cigarette. "I figure, same thing as you."

"How's she look?"

"Got too much of her daddy in her face to be what you'd call good looking." Dewey interrupted himself to deftly create a smoke sculpture, using his cigarette as an artist's tool to outline the curves of a female body. "Kinda hefty but mostly in the right places."

With a wave of his hand, Sonny swept away the smoky likeness. "Sounds good to me. You think her old man will get his bowels in an uproar if I talk to her?"

"What he don't know won't hurt him. She dated this Mexican catskinner a couple of times before he took off. Must've went back to Texas. I don't think her daddy ever found that out, so I guess she'll keep a secret."

"Introduce me."

"No way. I don't need no poor white trash with pillowcases over their heads coming around. She hangs around the Burger Barn after school. Bleached blonde, tight clothes, cigarette stuck in her mouth. Have at it. She won't be hard to talk to. Don't call her Frances, though. She likes to be called Farah."

"You want to go somewhere for a beer?"

"Sure." She hesitated. "But I'd need an ID."

"How old are you, anyway?"

Frances jutted her lower jaw forward. "Almost sixteen."

Sonny struck the steering wheel with both fists.

"It's okay. I started dating when I was thirteen." Frances moved her shoulders up and back. "Everybody says I look older than I am."

Sonny ran his eyes up and down Frances and nodded. "Yeah, you do. But fifteen is still fifteen."

Frances leaned toward Sonny and whispered into his ear. "I won't tell if you don't."

"Well, can we go somewhere and just talk? You know, get acquainted?"

"Sure."

"I don't know much about where to go."

"Let's go down to the strip pit."

"There's strip pits all over this county. Which one?"

"This is the one where all the kids go to park." Frances gave directions, moving her upraised hand to the left and right as she described each turn. "You go out Five Mile Road. You turn at this little store and go down this dirt road until you come to the strip pit." She nodded, then added a final detail. "This path goes down to the water but I like to park on this hill looking over it. Sometimes, you can see the moon reflected on the water. It's real pretty."

Sonny leaned close to the windshield and looked upward. "Well, there's not much of a moon but maybe we'll see some stars." He coaxed the V-8 into life, backed out of the Burger Barn parking lot, and drove away from Ebenezer.

Clarence Loomis was standing just inside the front door when his daughter entered the house. "Who brought you home?"

Frances stepped around her father. "Just a guy I met. He's nice."

Clarence followed his daughter from the foyer into the living room. "Is this one white?"

"Yes, Daddy, this one's white."

"Well, I couldn't see him too clear, what with him hiding in his car."

Frances turned to face her father. "He wasn't hiding. He even waited until I got to the door. Since you were spying on me, you saw that."

"How old is he?"

"He's only about twenty-something."

Clarence took a step closer to Frances. "Yeah, well, twenty-something is still too old for you to be going out with. Your mother never would've put up with your trampy ways."

"Whatever I know about being a tramp, I learned right here in this house."

Clarence placed his hands on his daughter's shoulders. "Angel." He attempted to draw her to him.

Frances spit a reply toward her father. "No." She jerked away from Clarence, collided with the sofa, nearly fell. "Leave me alone." Red-faced, she started toward the stairs.

Clarence shouted at the retreating figure of his daughter. "I don't want you seeing him any more. You got that?"

"Yes, sir, Daddy, sir." Frances charged up the stairs, her feet drumming on each carpeted step.

Sonny took his hand off the door handle of his car. "Makes sense. We can take turns driving." He slid into the passenger seat of Dewey's Camaro.

Dewey fired up the Camaro, which emitted a deep rumble and some blue smoke. "It's not far, down the highway toward Birmingham. You probably passed it when you came up here." Dewey steered the low-slung, bright red car onto the pavement and worked his way through the gears. "How'd it go with Farah? Get any?"

"We made out some, but that was it. You never told me she's fifteen."

"You said you liked the young stuff. Anyway, I expect ol' Pedro took care of her cherry."

"Fifteen's not just young, Fifteen's jailbait, irregardless of what your friend Pedro might've took care of. Besides, I got to see her old man about a job."

"Her kind don't tell their daddies nothing."

"Maybe not, but I need to get along up here, me being an ex-con and all."

"You never said what you were in for. If you don't mind me asking."

"No big thing. Started out to be a simple B and E. Who would've thought some old biddy with a walker would have her house wired? We got nailed coming out the back door."

"We?"

"My brother. He only got one year. His lawyer put it mostly on me, planning and all."

"Some brother." Dewey glanced at Sonny. "Sorry, I shouldn't have said that."

"It don't bother me much, any more. He's back in the lock-up. Out in Arizona." Sonny made himself busy with a cigarette.

The two-lane blacktop, a main highway by Nall County standards, snaked through an area that had been in an economic downturn for nearly 140 years. The tin-roofed share-cropper cabins had mostly disappeared into the kudzu, their occupants fled to urban slums, their hereditary lords buried in white Protestant graveyards. As Dewey and Sonny drove through the deep and deeper greens of rural underbelly that Nall County had long been, every mile took them past another strip pit, gaping wounds inflicted upon the earth by explosives and bulldozers. Old Creek and Scotch-Irish home places, burial grounds marked and unmarked, paths of social and commercial intercourse that had served for centuries, all had been sacrificed to the appetites of the industrial South. The overburden of earth had been shoved aside to lay bare the precious black seams, coal destined to be fed into the maws of the steel mills' coke ovens or the power company's generators.

After several miles, Dewey pulled off the pavement onto an expanse of red dirt that had been bulldozed clear of all vegetation. "His office is in that trailer. That's his Buick, so he's probably inside." Dewey parked and Sonny followed him into the trailer. Inside, Sonny remained silent while Dewey stepped toward an old wooden desk, behind which sat a compact white man with a face that spoke of sun and wind and rain. "Mr. Loomis, this is the guy I told you about, looking for a job."

"The one just out of Ashwater?"

Sonny took half a step forward and replied. "Yes, sir, I am."

"I see you somewhere, before?" Mr. Loomis tilted his head to one side and continued to study Sonny's face. "Before you did time, maybe?"

"No, sir, I doubt it. Before Ashwater, I did a coupla hitches in the army. Before that, I lived with my momma in Azalea Springs. I was born in Birmingham but we moved down there when I was a kid."

Clarence looked out the window. "We went to Azalea Springs for a vacation, the year before my wife died. Only time Maggie ever got to go to the beach. Your momma still down there?"

"No, sir. She died, right before I got out."

Clarence returned his gaze to Sonny. "They let you go to her funeral?"

"No, sir."

"That's a shame. They ought not treat a man that way, even in prison."

"No, sir. I try not to think about it. She did her best to be a good momma, though."

Clarence leaned back in his chair and crossed his arms. "Well, I believe in giving a man a second chance if he'll work hard. You look like you could heft a fifty-pound bag of ANFO. You willing to do what you're told? This ain't no easy job, and I don't take no laziness, no back-talk. Do I, Dewey?"

"No, sir, Mr. Loomis."

Sonny took another half-step forward. "Sir, I know I'm a stranger and an ex-con, but I'm not afraid of work."

"All right, but one mess-up and you're out of here. Sheriff Curbow's a good friend of mine. I intend to ask him to check you out. Buster Jones still the warden down at Ashwater?"

Sonny nodded. "Yes, sir."

"Well, if you check out okay, I could use you. I'm the certified blaster. Dewey does the drilling, you'll do the grunt work." Clarence looked down at the papers on his desk and began rearranging them.

"Thank you, sir."

Two days later, Sheriff Grady Curbow called to report that Sonny had drawn very little attention to himself during his stay at Ashwater State Prison. Warden Jones did recall that Sonny had some skills for building lawn furniture. Clarence hung up the telephone, found Dewey, and told him he wanted to see Sonny.

The following day, Clarence came to work early, as he usually did when the paperwork was beginning to pile up. He parked, entered the end of the trailer that served as his office, and went to work on the pile of forms waiting on his desk. About twenty minutes later, he glanced out the window and saw Sonny drive up with Dewey sitting beside him.

Clarence stared at the light blue Ford hardtop, noted the missing hubcap and the dent in the passenger-side door, all as clearly visible as it had been under the street light in front of his house. Clarence watched Dewey and Sonny get out of the car and head toward the other end of the trailer where there were some vending machines. Rising from his desk, he cracked the door in the partition separating the two parts of the trailer. He stood very still, listening.

Dewey led Sonny into the trailer. "Breakfast time, Mister Sonny."

"What they got?"

"Greasy sausage biscuits and stale crackers. Cold drinks in the other machine."

They purchased their breakfast and sat at an unpainted picnic bench. Each peeled the plastic wrappers from his food. Dewey grinned as Sonny laid open his sausage biscuit, bit the end off a packet of mustard, then squirted its contents onto the sausage. "You like a little sausage with your mustard?"

"One thing you learn about in Ashwater is what mustard and ketchup are for."

"You see Farah again last night?"

Sonny took a bite of his food, made a wry face, swallowed some Dr. Pepper. "Yeah, for what it's worth. I took her out to the strip pit and we messed around some. I figured booze would loosen her up, so I fed her that pint of vodka you loaned me. All that got loose was her tongue." Sonny lowered his voice. "She took to babbling, something about her daddy always rubbing up against her and putting his hands all over her. She said she had to lock the door to her room to keep him off of her."

"She said that? Keep him off of her?"

Sonny glanced over both shoulders. "Keep him off or keep him out. Something like that."

"I never woulda guessed. She say anything else?"

"Yeah. Said he watches her like a hawk." Sonny emitted a brief laugh, more of a snort. "I reckon that makes Mr. Loomis a chicken hawk. Anyway, she got to bawling about her momma being dead. After that, she puked her guts out and I took her home." He swallowed the last bite of his sausage biscuit. "I'm a fool, messing around with something that could put me back in the slam."

"You think Mr. Loomis has caught on that you're his competition?"

"I doubt it. I've never been to her house, except the first time we went out. I pick her up and drop her off at the Burger Barn."

Clarence waited until Dewey and Sonny had finished eating and were standing outside the trailer, smoking. Then, he closed the door between the two parts of the trailer, crossed his office to the outside door, and called Dewey into the trailer. "You think Sonny's ready to start humping ANFO?"

"Yes, sir, I do. He's got a good attitude. You want to start him today?"

"Might as well. Sheriff Curbow said he checked out okay. You ready to initiate him?"

Dewey laughed. "Absolutely, Mr. Loomis. We'll get him good, just like y'all got me. Third bag's the one. You going to watch?"

"Wouldn't miss it for the world. Soon as I check the ANFO and get back to the trailer, y'all can get busy."

Sonny was leaning against his Ford when Dewey and Clarence emerged from the trailer. Clarence, carrying a small wooden box, walked past Sonny without speaking and headed toward a five-ton truck parked about 100 yards away. Sonny pushed himself erect and watched Clarence for a moment. Then, he turned to Dewey. "What'd he say?"

"Said you're good to go."

Sonny raised his fist and punched the air. "Yeah. Where do I start?"

"We got to unload that explosives truck, soon as he checks the load. Come on. "

Sonny followed Dewey, his feet stirring up red dust that soon covered the well-worn work boots Dewey had loaned him. As they neared the truck, Clarence climbed down from the bed and began his return to the trailer. Sonny slowed, grinned, and nodded, but Clarence looked away and did not pause or respond. Sonny glanced over his shoulder at Clarence's retreating figure, then hurried to catch up with Dewey. "You know, I ought not be chasing after jailbait. I already done a nickel. Statutory's good for a dime, at least. Besides, her daddy gave me a job."

Dewey climbed into the bed of the truck. "Yeah, maybe you're right."

"Soon as I get me a day off, I'm goin' down to Birmingham. Maybe take Miss Janelle to a picture show or something." Sonny gripped the edge of the truck bed and prepared to swing himself up.

Dewey raised a hand. "No, you stay down there. I'll pass it down, you stack it on that pallet. Be real careful. This stuff is high explosive, you know."

Sheriff Curbow swung his long, skinny legs out of his air-conditioned patrol car and unfolded the rest of his six-foot-four frame. He stood with his head bowed, his hands resting on the gunbelt that girded his narrow hips. Having adjusted to the blast of heat, he strolled over to the five-ton truck. He stood, arms folded, looking back and forth, studying the way the bed had been lifted off the rear axle and shoved into the back of the cab. Then, he peered into the six-foot-deep crater behind the remains of the truck. He was shaking his head at the carnage when Clarence joined him. "Anybody killed?"

"Dewey. And this new guy, Sonny."

"What happened here, Clarence?"

Clarence shielded his eyes from the sun's glare and looked up at the sheriff. "Well, Dewey was playing a trick on Sonny. Dewey told Sonny to stack the ANFO on the pallet when he passed it down to him." Clarence pointed to the point in space where Dewey had stood, on the back of the truck. "Dewey handed down a couple of bags real careful, like it might blow up if it was handled too rough. That made Sonny nervous, like it was supposed to." Clarence now pointed toward the crater where the pallet had been. "Sonny stacked those fifty-pound bags like he was stacking crates of eggs. Then, with the third bag, Dewey acted like he tripped and throwed it up in the air so it would fall right next to Sonny. The last I saw of Sonny was him yelling and jumping out of the way. Then, everything was blowed all to hell and gone."

"This the Sonny you had me check on?"

"That's him. Was him."

"Red-headed? Drove that blue Ford over yonder?" The sheriff nodded toward the trailer. "Staying at Dewey's place?"

"That's the one. Sounds like you checked him out real good."

The sheriff returned his gaze to Clarence. "That's what you asked me to do. Clarence, I also saw Frances get into his car and go somewhere with him. Looked to me like they were headed out toward that strip pit where all the kids go. You know about that?"

"She mentioned it. Can't say I approved but you know how it is. Kids will be kids. I don't think it was anything serious."

Sheriff Curbow continued to study Clarence's face for a long moment. "If you say so. Where's the bodies?"

"We couldn't find hardly any of Sonny. He was blowed to bits. See those blackbirds? That's little pieces of Sonny they're pecking at. Dewey's over yonder in the ambulance, waiting for you to look at him. He stayed more or less in one piece, except that his head was blowed off, along with his right hand."

"How the hell did this happen? Is ANFO all that sensitive?"

"Not normally. It's not supposed to blow except with primer and a cap. I've seen that trick played a dozen times. All the other times, the new guy just jumped out of his skin and then stood around looking goofy because we fooled him. It was always funny, before."

The sheriff removed his Stetson, smoothed his thin, white hair, then replaced the hat. "Whose idea was it?"

Clarence thought for a moment, then looked toward the ambulance. "Dewey suggested it, but I didn't see nothing wrong with it."

"Where'd the ANFO come from?"

"Straight from the supplier. This is their truck."

Sheriff Curbow moved closer to the truck and stretched to look into the bed. "Was anybody messing with it before they started unloading it?"

Clarence followed the sheriff but did not attempt to look into the truck bed. "Not that I saw. I counted the bags and check everything out, like always. It's part of my job."

"This is mighty peculiar. Y'all got any other kinds of explosives around here?"

"There's primer and caps, but they're kept separate. Even with all three parts together, just dropping it six or seven feet wouldn't cause an explosion. The cap needs an electrical pulse to go off. Primer is normally as stable as ANFO."

Sheriff Curbow looked more directly at Clarence. "What's that mean, 'normally?'"

"In the summertime, when it's hot, it's not a good idea to let primer sit out too long." Clarence turned toward the trailer. "Speaking of hot, we ought to get out of this sun. Let's get a cold drink."

Sheriff Curbow did not move. "Why's it not a good idea to let primer sit in the sun?"

Clarence took a deep breath. "Primer is gel and sawdust in a stick. When it's real hot, gel can liquefy and leak out. By itself, gel is kinda unstable. So, in hot weather, we store the primer in a refrigerator and use it as soon as we take it out." He placed a hand on the sheriff's arm and spoke with increased deliberation. "Grady, the whole point is, they were only handling ANFO."

"Yeah, okay." The sheriff removed his sun glasses, wiped

some sweat from them, then returned them to their perch on his nose. "You reckon this was some kind of black and white thing? Over Sonny and Dewey hanging around together?"

Clarence shook his head. "That's no problem on this job. Klan, maybe? I always wondered, maybe the Klan ran off that Mexican catskinner we had."

Sheriff Curbow stood, looking down into the crater, reflecting. "I don't know nothing about your disappeared catskinner, but I doubt this is Klan doings. Anything more complicated than a Zippo is over their heads." He turned his back to the crater and walked to where his deputies were stringing yellow plastic tape around the accident site. "Tape off a bigger area. The state forensics guys are gonna insist on looking at everything. The state mine inspectors will probably come out, maybe the feds, too." He picked up a small stone and threw it toward the blackbirds. Two of the birds lifted briefly into the air, cawed angrily, then returned to their feeding. "Chase them damn blackbirds off, they're gobbling up the evidence. If y'all find any pieces of Sonny, bag 'em and tag 'em. Clarence, I'll take that cold drink now."

Clarence bought the sheriff a Pepsi, then waited around while the sheriff took a look at Dewey. As soon as the sheriff left, Clarence got into his Buick and drove toward Ebenezer. He did not turn onto his street. Instead, he passed through town, drove out Five Mile Road, turned at a little store, and drove down a dirt road to an old strip pit. After he left the pavement, he drove no more than twenty miles per hour and took great pains to avoid bumps in the road. At the strip pit, he parked atop a hill, got out of his car, and opened the trunk. He opened a wooden box and withdrew from it a small bottle that had been nestled in cotton. Taking very precise steps, he walked down a path that led to the water's edge. He bent over and slowly, carefully poured the contents of the bottle into the muddy water. Then, he threw the empty bottle far out into the pit, returned to his car, and drove away.

Returning, the Buick kicked up a hanging plume of dust and slammed through the bumps. At the store, Clarence spun the steering wheel and lurched onto the pavement without looking for traffic. Staring down the on-rushing ribbon of asphalt, he told himself how much better it had been, after the catskinner was taken care of and Frances left her door open for several weeks. When he passed the sign that declared *Here We Raised Our Ebenezer*, he voiced aloud his prayer that, in her grief over Sonny's death, his sweet little angel would again turn to him for comfort.

Posters

SEE THE WORLD

"Don't you have a bed?"

It began with glances over espresso. She laughed when I winked. I laughed at her laughter. We strolled along the quay. She pointed to the gray ladies and I told her about their bloodlines and their particular charms—there, a British destroyer with Sea Darts, there, a French frigate with Exocets, farther out in the harbor, my cruiser with Tomahawks and Harpoons. She said they were sinister sisters but I let that pass. At noon, she showed me how to dip bread in olive oil. When I asked where we could go next, she ran her fingertips along my forearm and said we could go to her apartment.

The only visible furniture was a dark, hulking table, accompanied by three equally stern chairs. After I had been there a couple of times, Simone told me that a comrade had broken the fourth chair into clubs, useful in political discussions. The posters on the pale walls hurled forth the likes of *Red Guards Advance against Capitalists* and *Workers of the World Unite*. The marble parquet floor was hard and cool through the soles of my sneakers, despite the softly blazing Greek sunshine outside. There was a closed door, maybe a bedroom, but I was never to know.

"Beds are for sleeping. Pleasure is enhanced by pain. You are a soft American."

"Yeah, but…"

Simone tugged at my zipper, cleared my mind of protest. We made love on the floor, then went to sit at the table. I put my skivvies on but Simone left her clothes where she'd dropped them. She slouched in her chair, her legs apart as if to cool herself. One elbow rested on the table, a smoldering Karelia Plain Oval gripped lightly between her thumb and forefinger. Her eyes, their luster already heightened by sex, filled with amusement at my attempt to rub some relief into my bruised knees. "Did we not have marvelous sex?"

I couldn't permit the triumph in her voice to pass unchallenged. "I could've had marvelous sex without the marble floor."

"Not with me, you couldn't." Simone stood and turned away, leaving me to fear I had spoiled the moment. Then, she took a bottle of Tsantali and a couple of unmatched glasses from a windowsill, sat, and began pouring. "Don't worry. Equality is a core tenet. Next time, my knees get banged up." She sat the larger glass of ouzo before me. "Do we have time, before you return to your ship?"

SOUTHSIDE

I spent the first year after I got out of the navy in Birmingham, remembering Simone and working as a poster boy. I wasn't one of those photogenic studs whose likeness convinces the masses that they, too, will look sexy smoking a Marlboro or a Kool. I was the kind of poster boy who hangs posters. In my native South, boy does not allude solely to age. It can be a pejorative that signifies a man's place at the bottom of the socioeconomic order. I've witnessed men in their fifties, broom or rake in hand, being addressed as boy. I was twenty-six and once a petty officer on a ship of the line, but I spent nearly twelve months answering to poster boy.

My job was to put up posters anywhere a public space could

be violated for the sake of cause or commerce. Causes ran from *Salvation Now* to *Don't Pollute*. Commerce ranged from *Two for the Price of One* to *Vote for Joe Blow*. I held American politics to be commerce, not cause, a notion Simone planted in my head. On the other hand, I held *Saint Hildegard Sodality Barbecue Here or to Go* to be more cause than commerce. I never did make up my mind about *I Want to Buy the World a Coke*.

I had originally wanted to ship over, to reenlist for what would have been my third hitch in the US Navy. All I wanted to do was cross-deck, transfer from my homeport-bound ship to anything headed back to the Mediterranean. That way, I would have another chance of pulling liberty in Greece. Greece, where a hard-shelled communist with a soft center had insisted on practicing the pleasure through pain principle beneath her favorite poster. It was all alone on one wall, like a shrine, the black-on-red image of the eternally proselytizing Argentine. All we needed to complete a Marxist fantasy was *Bandiera Rossa* or some such playing stridently in the background. Even without the music, it was rollicking tenderness on what had been the floor of an ancient temple dedicated to some member of a forgotten pantheon. It was the most exotic and erotic combination of things hard and things soft I ever experienced or ever expect to experience.

It was the command master chief who ratted me out to the executive officer, telling him I had fallen in with reds and could no longer be trusted in the message center of a guided missile cruiser. I guess he figured I would pass on to Simone, who would pass on to The Evil Empire, the secrets encrypted in our skipper's birthday greeting to the chief of naval operations. The XO advised the skipper not to pass a potential spy, maybe an already spy, to an unsuspecting Med-bound skipper. The Annapolis types look out for each other. So, the skipper said no way to my cross-deck request and told the chief to tell me, which he seemed to greatly enjoy doing, that he was reconsidering my request to ship over. I decided, to hell with the navy, I'll get out, go home, and reap the education benefits of the GI Bill.

Which I did, after a year of going around Birmingham with a pastepot and whatever posters my employer contracted to print and distribute. I didn't go straight to college because, in her only letter to me, Simone said she wanted me to return to Greece, only please wait until she said it was okay, and it definitely had to be after the elections. She was running for parliament and didn't want her opponents to make an issue of her liaison with an American. I didn't want to quit school in the middle of a semester, and I knew damn well I'd be off to Greece as soon as Simone said so—I even went to the Federal Building and got a passport—so I put off starting school until the Simone thing played out.

Simone answered none of my eight letters. I read in *The Birmingham News* that Simone's Trotskyite faction was blown out in the elections. Reading that led me to remember how, one day while we were sipping ouzo and recharging my batteries— Simone's batteries were always on full charge—she told me I was a lackey of the CIA because my ship's message center was passing intelligence reports on the communists and, therefore, I was part of a capitalist plot to subvert the people. I told her that was bullshit, whereupon she assumed a very European air of superiority and informed me that I had not been educated to understand these matters. That was not totally untrue but it pissed me off, anyway, and there was no more sex, that day. After reading about how Simone lost out on her shot at parliament, I had to tell myself that maybe she wasn't writing because she thought I'd given her only letter, which included some typical Simone stuff about her conservative opponent being a neofascist, to the CIA. That was totally insane, but commies are big on conspiracy theories.

So, during my year of coming to terms with Simone's silence, while still remembering how she and I would take turns leaving sweaty butt-prints on that memorable marble floor, I plastered posters all over Birmingham, but mostly on Southside, which is more of a poster kind of place. Once, I did go out of state, to Azalea Springs, Mississippi, to do the publicity for a big holy roller temple fund raiser, which they were building in defiance of the Gulf Coast casinos. It was a first-class production, with four-color posters promising *Jesus in the Face of the Moneychangers*. I had always thought that particular biblical allusion was to bankers, not gamblers, but maybe that's putting too fine a point on things. Anyway, it must have worked. I heard they collected nearly a quarter-million toward raising their cathedral.

But, like I said, mostly I worked Southside. The problem— maybe it was only a problem for me, maybe not for anybody else—was that the good poster places already had posters posted, often by me. That meant, for example, an investment opportunity that sounded like a rip-off might get plastered over a grainy picture of an overweight teenage girl with a plea for information, *Any Information No Questions Asked Small Reward*. Or, *Meat and Two Vegetables For $4.95* might hide *Meat and Three Vegetables plus Tea for $3.95*, solely because it was posted a week later. When I complained about this, my boss, who had been in the business for about fifty years, said I was only a poster boy with a lot to learn. He said, if I worked the same space long enough, the order of things would reverse, and reverse again. He said it was all business for him and a job for me.

But, some of Simone's fist-in-the-air lectures had stuck in the back of my mind and kept telling me it was unfair. Some needs are greater, some causes are more just, some offers are a better deal for the people. Yes, for the people. Still, I liked the job. I liked being outdoors, after nearly eight years in a cramped message center with piped-in air. I also liked the money. My boss paid by the piece and, if I wanted to shift into an acquisitive Republican gear and really bust my ass, I could earn about as much as the writer I hoped to someday be.

So, I came up with my own way of inserting a little justice into the process. What I did was, any time I put a poster over one I judged superior in some way, I would figure out how to support the bargain or entreaty I was about to render unseen. I made a point of eating at the meat-and-three for $3.95 and I took a couple of friends. I made an anonymous donation to the grandparents of the missing girl so they could pay for more posters for me to put up. One time, I even went to a tent meeting but I kept my rear end firmly planted on the bench when the choir invited me to *Stand Up, Stand Up for Jesus*.

A TERMINAL CASE OF SWEETNESS

And that's how I met Elaine. Elaine's poster offered a *String Quartet Performing a Classic Medley*, playing at this highfalutin liberal arts college to raise money for AIDS. Elaine, pictured on the poster with the other three, was the cellist. Even in the lousy, black-and-white poster picture, she looked as wholesome and winsome as one of the Doublemint Twins. I had never heard—had never heard of, for that matter—a string quartet, nor had I given much thought to the AIDS epidemic. But, before I coated Elaine with paste and covered her with *Get E-Mail Absolutely Free by Signing up Just Five New Customers*, I jotted down the particulars of her performance and stuck it in my pocket with the rest of that day's accumulation of good deals and worthy causes.

Now, I'm about to start my third year in the creative writing program at the University of Alabama in Birmingham. Hanging all those posters provided me with more than room and board. They provided me with half a dozen good story lines, one of which, about a revival preacher struggling with his homosexuality, made me a finalist for the Pushcart Prize. That's pretty damn good for a sophomore.

Elaine is finishing her masters in music at Ole Miss. She now spends her weekends with me, breaking her mother's heart and enraging her father, who was right in thinking she was still a virgin when she met me. I could tell him she resisted my lustful advances for more than a year, but I doubt that would make him feel any better. Pretty, proper Elaine. Elaine, whose shoes are always in season. Elaine, who would be mystified by the idea of arriving at pleasure through pain and appalled at how that might be accomplished, but who has never suspected me of being a CIA stooge. Sweet, predictable Elaine.

For a long time, I hardly ever thought about Simone. Then, one Saturday afternoon while we were lounging around my apartment—Elaine had cookies in the oven, her favorite after-sex activity—she asked me about other women. I guess she figured I owed her that, in return for the great gift of her chastity. I tried to escape the question with a shrug, but my rush of memories must have made its way to my face. She removed the arm I had draped around her shoulders and repeated the question. I mumbled something about youthful flings and went into the kitchen for a beer. When I returned to the couch, Elaine asked if it had been in Greece. I nodded and turned the TV on. Elaine captured the remote control, pressed the mute button, and asked if it had been an older woman. I was so startled by Elaine's insight, I confessed. Yes, the woman in Greece had been older, but that was all behind me now. When I asked Elaine what made her think that, she said she could sense I had been with a more exciting and more experienced woman. I told Elaine she was exciting enough, and the way I felt about her had nothing to do with experience. Elaine extended one very rigid little finger and punched the mute button. It was the only time she ever asked about other women.

A couple of months before the end of last semester, Elaine declared it would be great fun to rub elbows with real, live Yankees and see some musicals. Her folks pitched a hissy fit about it but we went anyway. Elaine really does love me.

One of the first things I noticed was that New York's posters reflect New York's self-anointment as a world-class capital of culture and commerce and everything else. Theater ads cover more than Broadway or off-Broadway, they also tout productions in London and Buenos Aires. Airfare specials are just as likely to be offered by Lufthansa or Cathay Pacific as by Delta or United. Causes range from saving whales and/or tigers to freeing Tibet and/or Cuba.

LATTÉ

Elaine came out of the shower, fully freshened, a towel tightly wrapped from her armpits to her knees. She asked if I liked the two hundred dollars per ounce scent she had bought that morning at Bergdorf's. It occurred to me I don't know how the real Elaine smells. She is always inside this almost-visible cloud of toiletries—cologne and deodorant and mouthwash and whatever else the merchants of illusion require. Then, my writer's brain added conflict to the plot. I remembered the smells of Simone—a hint of sweat in her sun-warmed hair, a hint of garlic from her lips, a hint of her private musk as she lifted her dress over her head. Simone never practiced olfactory deceit. I told Elaine she smelled nice.

Elaine pecked me on the cheek, then went to the desk and began rustling the theater pages of the *New York Times*. I knew that, if I didn't come up with something else, I was in for another over-priced extravaganza. So, I launched a preemptive strike. "Okay, we've done *Cats* and *Phantom of the Opera*. How about, let's go to a Greenwich Village coffee shop?"

Elaine made a little-girl handclap. "Yes! Do you know of one?"

"No, but that'll be part of the fun. Let's just take a taxi to the middle of Greenwich Village and then discover."

"We could do that, I suppose." Elaine paused. She was not through supposing. "A friend told me about a place with poetry reading that brews an excellent latté. The proprietors are Puerto Rican expatriates. Shall we try it?"

"Elaine, Puerto Ricans aren't expatriates. They're US citizens."

"Oh." Elaine tightened her lips.

"You're right, that's not important. Sure, let's go there."

At the coffee shop, Elaine assumed that, since her politically-challenged friend had suggested the place, she was in charge. "Latté, dos, por favor."

The guy with the ponytail slapped his left hand on the bar, lifted his right with two fingers extended, and replied in pure Cajun. "Café au lait, twice, coming right out, cher."

While our latté was being brewed, I walked around the room, inhaled the aromas of strong coffee and steamed milk, squinted through the carefully contrived coffee house gloom at the posters. There were dozens of them, the fresher ones partially covering others that were yellowed and curling.

"Looking for more story ideas, dear?"

"Yeah, I guess. Look at this one. What d'you think it says?"

Elaine joined me. "*Raw Poetry Howl.* I imagine it's some sort of poetry reading. Tonight. Shall we stay for it?"

"No, I mean, underneath. The one that's almost covered up."

Elaine turned her attention to the protruding corner of the nearly covered poster. "Well, let's see. Free something. Difficult to say." She leaned closer. "Free, then it looks like L and A. La. Free latté, perhaps?" Elaine frowned and stepped back from the puzzle. "That's wishful thinking, of course. I give up. *Raw Poetry Howl* is covering too much of it."

I reached out and picked at the corner of *Raw Poetry Howl* with a fingernail. "Let's see."

"Darling! We don't even know these people."

"Sure we do. El Ponytail is a Puerto Rican expatriate from Louisiana. Anyway, the best story is underneath. It always is." I peeled back *Raw Poetry Howl*. The gloom made reading difficult, but it spared Elaine the contortions of surprise, then understanding, then horror I felt gripping my face. She nodded when I mumbled something about taking a few notes.

"Please don't be too long. Our latté is ready. I'll be at our table."

La Greca

Free La Greca. La Pasionaria of the New Millennium, the poster explained, was an *International Revolutionary* who'd been *Imprisoned in South America While Fighting for the Freedom of the Oppressed*. There was no mention of how Simone came to be in South America or what act had led to her being thrown into the bowels of a municipal prison. In the picture, apparently a mugshot, La Greca, Simone, looked as though something had been worn out of her. There were shadows under her eyes that could have been smeared printer's ink but I knew were the results of pain unaccompanied by pleasure. Her untamed black curls were jammed into a beret like the one Che wore as he looked out, over the fierce coupling of the daughter of the proletariat and the imperialist warmonger, into a future he strove to influence but would never see.

Elaine does not know about the check made out to the La Greca Defense Fund, or that I asked to be kept informed of La Greca's fate.

I still have my passport.

Where Sin Lies

"Four dead of it this year alone." Bridie MacUlhaney jerked a cane chair back from the table, its hand-carved legs performing a brief thumping dance on the bare wooden floor. Seated, she crossed herself, mumbled a few words, then spooned butter beans onto her plate. "Lettin'em get away with it, that's a sin." The ferocious judgment in her tight glittering eyes belied her eighty years and ninety pounds.

Lonny MacUlhaney took the remaining butter beans. He did not return thanks. He gulped down mouthfuls of butter beans and fatback, sopped up the juice with his last bit of cornbread, pushed back from the table. "I'm going down to the union hall."

Mrs. MacUlhaney held her tongue until her grandson had walked the length of the three in-line rooms of their house but her words caught up with him. "Your father, God rest his soul, would've done what's right."

Lonny planted his scuffed brogans on the porch's edge. Thirty-two years earlier, he'd watched the broad back and confident step of Conor MacUlhaney, his father, on his way to the Number Nine shaft. Lonny looked up the empty street for a long moment, then stepped into the night and felt the frosted dead-brown weeds crunch beneath his feet. The weeds had long since taken over the flower beds planted by his mother the spring she died giving birth to his sister. The elder Mrs. MacUlhaney continued to tend the flowers after Kathleen's death, said they were for little Peggy. But after Conor died as

94

her husband had, beneath a dark mountain, Bridie turned away from beauty.

Lonny gathered about himself a faded field jacket with darker patches on the sleeves where sergeant's stripes and a 29th Infantry Division crest had been. He turned left down the street and aimed himself toward a dim point of light, the single bulb over a door at the far end of the street. He walked past a dozen shotgun-style company houses identical to the one he and his grandmother occupied.

The miners had built the union hall but the coal company had final authority over its presence within the compound. It was as sparse as the homes of the members, some unpainted tables and chairs, a pot-bellied iron stove. A rough box inside the door contained short lengths of oak, stout firewood that could also serve to knock knots on the heads of scabs.

Several men, from late teens to nearly sixty, clustered around the stove, their coats open so their flannel shirts could absorb the heat. The oldest man spoke as Lonny entered. "The Grievance Committee is assembled. You still for it, Lonny Mac?"

Lonny stroked the barbs sprouting from a cheek crazed by the eruptions of youth and the furrows of underground aging. "I reckon." He grinned. "Mamaw says I'm a sinner if I'm not."

"That old woman knows which side she's on. Where she came from, if she'd been a man she would've been a Molly Maguire."

Lonny nodded. "They say my papaw was both. What's the plan, Abel?"

Abel placed a motion before the assembly. "I'll go to the company office. Tomorrow, after we're done with things down here."

Lonny nodded. "I'm off at three. I'll go to the church, talk to the preacher." He glanced around the room at a dozen survivors of cave-in and lay-off. Each man bobbed his head, once.

On his way home, Lonny detoured past the church cemetery. In the wan moonlight, he could just make out the four graves added since April. Nearest the church was Patrick Jones, sent home by County General to cough out his lungs. Next to Patrick, an open grave awaited Patrick, Junior. PJ had made it to twelve before the omnipresent coal dust drove his asthma out of control three months after his father died. Farther back, near the MacUlhaney plot with its three headstones, were Mr. and Mrs. Jenkins, he taken in the same way as Patrick Jones, she by opening a vein the day after her husband's funeral. Lonny shoved his hands deeper into his pockets and turned away.

Reverend Calvert stood. Once a tall man, age and condition had bent him in the middle. The same gravities had required the flesh of his face to sag in sallow folds. He waved toward a straight-backed chair in front of his wooden desk. "You're not a member of this congregation, are you?"

Lonny accepted the chair. "My grandmother's Catholic. She says I'm lapsed. I came here once with Sarah Jenkins, before she left for California."

Reverend Calvert lowered himself into his chair. "What can I do for you?"

"I've been studying on sin. I figured to ask an expert."

Reverend Calvert exhaled a rush of dry air laced with humor. "If anybody knows about sin, it ought to be a preacher. What's your question?"

"If I lie, have I sinned?"

Reverend Calvert leaned back in his chair, causing its aged bones to creak. His body settled into a black suit that had matured to hints of bottle fly green, a suit tailored with a shorter, heavier man in mind. The frayed, bleach-weakened threads of his shirt were held together by heavy starch. His black tie was carefully knotted but set askew, as if to mitigate against any remaining suspicion of sartorial adequacy. "It depends."

"Depends on whether or not I get caught?"

Reverend Calvert employed a middling ration of righteous thunder. "Sinners always get caught in the end. It depends on the purpose of the lie."

"There's good lies and bad lies?"

"So to speak. Say you lie to evil to protect innocence. That's not a sin. Now, say—"

Lonny interrupted. The rasp of his voice escaped the preacher's sanctum and reverberated around the white-washed sanctuary. His words echoed among wooden pews rough-sanded by decades of denim and fine-buffed by a thousand yards of flour sacking laboriously stitched into Sunday best. The sound was absorbed by the pile of ragged hymnals behind the pine-board pulpit. "The sin is to lie to the innocent for evil purposes."

"Exactly. Sin lies in a sinner's heart."

Lonny stood, faltered, slapped two grimy palms down on the marred brown surface separating him from the preacher. The exertion jarred something loose within him. A fit of hacking mottled his pale complexion. He shuddered himself straight and began pacing between his chair and the desk. He raked his fingers through graying hair dank with November afternoon rain and the black effluvia that blanketed the dead earth of the valley. "So, I'm guilty of sin if I lie and harm those that trust me?"

Reverend Calvert swiveled his chair away from the sight and sound of Lonny, shifted his eyes to the window at the back of the office. "I've got to get ready for a funeral, Mr. McIlhenny."

Lonny stopped pacing. "MacUlhaney. My name's Londergan MacUlhaney." He spelled out both names, pausing between each letter. "Londergan after my mother's people. Papaw MacUlhaney brought his family here—"

"I reckon it's an interesting story, but I need—"

"From Pennsylvania by way of West Virginia. They say he was a Hibernian, one step ahead of the Pinkertons. Answer the question."

Lonny's tone quelled any further protest by the preacher. "What was it?"

"Is it a sin to lie to folks who trust you?"

Reverend Calvert took a breath. "Yes. Did you lie to somebody who trusts you?"

"Say it wasn't me. Say it was a company boss."

Reverend Calvert returned his gaze to Lonny. "I've heard tell of union grievances against the company. They say the company's hard on agitators. Did they lie to you?"

"I never said that. That was just an example."

"Why was this lie told?"

Lonny collapsed onto his chair. "For money."

"Did you, or somebody, lie for money?"

"Well, if somebody did, shouldn't he feel guilty?"

Reverend Calvert nodded. "Feeling guilt is the first step toward redemption. That's something to pray about." He pushed back the black and white encasement of his rawboned left wrist and glanced at a wristwatch heavy with gold. He tapped the unblemished crystal of the timepiece. "Look, Mr. MacUlhaney, it's getting late and I'm burying the Jones boy tomorrow. We can talk some other time."

Lonny stood, went to the door, returned bearing a leather pouch he'd dropped there when he arrived. "Here's the guilt to be prayed on." He upended the pouch over the desk. "Here's some mail, preacher. Straight from the post office, compliments of my cousin." He coughed, spewed whatever escaped his open mouth in Reverend Calvert's direction, selected a large envelope and ripped it open. "This one's mine.

Look. A government report on black lung, like the one my sister says you never returned to the library." Lonny stuffed the report back into his bag, picked up a folded newspaper, waved it at Reverend Calvert. "Look at this headline: *Reverend Calvert Assures Community Mines Pose No Health Risk.*" He dropped the newspaper and seized a beige envelope with an address window. "This one's for you." He hurled it at the preacher's head. "Your check from the coal company. Right on time. Like every month."

Reverend Calvert lifted himself from his chair. He stood at the window, his hands on either side of it. He looked out at the cemetery, at how the lengthening shadow of a pine darkened the grave awaiting PJ. "What do you want?"

Lonny lifted the bag and slipped its strap over his shoulder. "I want you to come with me. There's some miners down at the union hall wanting to speak with you about lies and sin."

Malfunction Junction

5:23 p.m. I-65 down Red Mountain, north into Birmingham and the intersection with I-20, nearing the crawl of traffic backed up by Malfunction Junction. At the Junction, nothing is ever as it should be. The surface is uneven and there are too few lanes. The exits are confusing—some left, some right, all poorly marked. If any roads in Jefferson County are rain-slicked, they are at the Junction. The sky over most of Alabama may be sunny blue, but over the Junction it will be the brown-gray of exhaust. Normally decent people grip their steering wheels with sweaty hands and push ahead of other citizens, risk death and destruction for the least advantage. They do this because they are passing through the open-air netherworld of Malfunction Junction. Breathe in the filth of the Junction, feel it erode the flesh and the spirit time after time, and it has to have some permanent caustic effect on the brain and on the soul.

Today, at the Junction, the traffic is the usual late-afternoon mix of eighteen-wheelers, junkmobiles, and fleets of oversized sports utility vehicles. Ahead, in a left exit lane, the driver of a Land Behemoth is so engrossed in cell phoning his stock broker he fails to notice the brakelightless 1973 Pontiac Bonneville at a dead stop in front of him. God only knows why the Bonneville's poor white trash driver chose to stop right here, right now. Their kind answer only to their higher power, who speaketh in tongues.

Between me and the two vehicles with their bumpers now intertwined, there's a great white van shaped like a space shuttle, driven by this dufus who's gotten himself trapped in the far-left Tuscaloosa exit lane when he needs to be in the far-right Atlanta exit lane. He's driving a space ship clone, but this guy's no rocket scientist. Malfunction Junction has claimed another hapless victim.

The Junction will not hold me in its grip today. I know its tricks. I spot the jam in time to move over one lane, inserting myself behind a smoke-snorting transfer truck and ahead of a teenager driving an immaculate, bright red Monte Carlo with wheels that cost more than the car and speakers that fill the back seat. The teenager casts a practiced glare of intimidation into my rear-view mirror. He'd think twice about messing with me if he knew about the hand cannon in the glove box, the one Daddy insisted on giving me when I lived in Southside because he was certain my neighbors were drug dealers. Actually, some of them were, but not the dangerous kind. The teenager cranks his volume up to the point where it makes the pavement around him vibrate. I guess he thinks making himself deaf will somehow punish me for pushing ahead of him.

Unlike the dufus, I've avoided being trapped behind the minor collision occupying the Tuscaloosa exit lane. His passenger, serving as his navigator, has her window down and is leaning out, the better to assess the possibilities of wedging into the long line of uncaring vehicles in my lane. As she looks back and forth, I come alongside the van.

Her fine, fair features, surrounded by a wealth of brunette hair are, surely, attributes of superior breeding, at least three generations of First Circle sorority. Lovely, and intelligent, because that sort of breeding does not produce fools. Her eyes are green and clear and, perhaps, a bit wider than they would usually be. She deserves better than being with her dufus at Malfunction Junction. Her eyes tell me she's not angry, or panicked, or defeated, just a bit concerned about how to control the dufus. She's in no way needful of pity. She offers no self-deprecating grin, no helpless shrug of her shoulders, no mouthing of pleading words. She maintains her dignity. She simply looks into my eyes for a split second, across pavement stained by the oil leaks of countless 1973 Bonnevilles.

The grim anger of this place diminishes within me. She is not compelled by the Junction and I need not be, not today. I slow down and nod her ahead. The dufus jerks through a stop-and-go maneuver, dashing ahead for a few feet, then slamming on his brakes, while he struggles to understand his navigator's directions. Finally, he gets it right, veers around the Dreadnought, swoops ahead of me and across the traffic. Dufus is as dufus does.

Her hand, slim and delicate but surely stronger than it looks, extends from the passenger-side window. Her wrist bent to just the right angle for the gesture, her long fingers gracefully akimbo, she signals far more than gratitude. With a simple, brief wave of her exquisite hand, she tells me she knows I opened the way for her out of the Junction. That she's on her way to Atlanta with the dufus is no matter. She knows my heart.

And, I know their license plate number.

I could slow down, swing in behind them, follow them eastward. The impulse is visceral. It tells me to act while there's still time, give her a choice. No. This is not the time. This will play out, but not now.

5:24. I exit onto I-20 westbound and hurry away from Malfunction Junction. A couple of miles later, I descend to the surface world of four-room bungalows with chain link fences and yard art. This is Daddy's little world. I'm in time for supper in front of the TV, watching the local news. Daddy doesn't like the murder reports, so he clicks the volume down when the talking head gets to the latest shooting. "Les Parker can't play dominoes without telling me his grandchildren make straight A's."

"You need another slice of onion, Daddy?"

"No, thanks. Then, he asks how old you are and if you're married yet."

"You tell him it's none of his business?"

"Next, he has to know if you've got yourself a permanent job yet."

Foolishly, I think it might make him feel better if I tell him about my encounter. "I saw a girl I'd like to meet, on my way over here."

He sits up a little straighter. "Yeah?"

I describe the woman in the white van.

Daddy's eyes start jumping around, the way they do when he is trying to connect his thoughts with my words. "Wait a minute. Where did you meet her?"

This was a mistake. I don't have enough energy to lie my way out of it. "I didn't actually meet her. I saw her at Malfunction Junction."

Daddy slumps back into his recliner and drops his chin onto his chest. "This is just some more of your dreaming."

After that, we retreat into our usual silence. I serve myself another helping of banana pudding and we watch two sit-coms about families with a mob of kids. Grateful that Daddy goes to bed immediately after the Lawrence Welk rerun, I leave.

9:05. Back on I-20. At Malfunction Junction, instead of bearing right onto I-65, I continue eastbound on I-20. Despite the thicker traffic that always clogs the Junction, I maintain my speed and blast right through. I scarcely notice the blue light flashing in front of a pulled-over pickup. The Junction will not delay me or distract me, not tonight. I do need gas for the drive to Atlanta, so I exit and pull into a discount filling station. I finish pumping, then go inside to pay and pee. The rest room door is locked, so I wait. It occurs to me there may be some kind of problem, so I knock.

The response is muffled. "Get off the door, man."

I don't know what to say, so I just wait. After a couple of minutes, the door swings open, belching a cloud of smoke containing a skinny, shirtless white guy, maybe in his early twenties. His undershorts extend a good six inches above the waistband of his filthy jeans. Perched atop his straggly yellow curls is a black baseball cap, worn backwards. My guess is, he's one of the trolls that seek shelter beneath the bridges of Malfunction Junction.

"You the one banging on the door?"

I step back and avoid eye contact. He saunters past my silence, toward the cash register, while I enter the rest room. I relieve myself, then step to the wash basin and discover that the troll has defecated in it.

I hold my breath until I'm out of the rest room, then I breath deep to keep the puke down. I turn toward the cashier's counter. The troll is still at the register. Now, I can see the words above the backwards-pointed bill of his cap: ROCKIT SCIENTIST. "Hey, you."

The troll turns. "You talkin' to me?"

"You left a mess in there."

"So what?"

Good question. He's probably got a knife in his pocket. "Nothing." I step around him and hand a twenty to the cashier. The troll's a foot away, glaring into my ear, smelling like used beer. The other one, two years ago, the black punk with the dreadlocks, had smelled that way when he bent over me. That time, I lay there like a hurt rabbit and begged him not to shoot me again. He laughed and jerked my wallet out of my hand. He even called 911 on my cell phone, which he also stole. He said he was finished with me, come and pick up the garbage.

I crawled to my car to get Daddy's gun, but the ambulance arrived and the punk was gone, anyway.

I bolt before the cashier can make change. I get into my car. I reach into the glove box and remove the .357. My hands are shaking, but I manage to check the cylinder. Ready for action.

I get out of my car and head toward the door of the filling station. I must be walking, but I cannot feel my feet striking the ground. I may not be breathing, because my throat is closed and my chest feels tight. I can see straight ahead, but the edges are closed in and blurry.

The troll comes out of the filling station and steps into my vision tunnel. There's something in his hand, and he's lifting it toward me. I cock the pistol as I swing it up and point it at him. He's saying something but I'm already pulling the trigger. It's the first time I've fired the pistol and I'm not prepared for the noise or the recoil. I'm jolted backward and I get a ringing in my ears. I realize my eyes are closed, so I open them.

The troll is kneeling, clutching his gut. On the pavement in front of him, where he's dropped it, is my change. I pick it up, because it's six dollars. I have to put him out of his misery. I walk behind him and blow the I out of ROCKIT on his stupid cap.

I get back on I-20. The troll was here so I could prove I'll do whatever's necessary. It all fits. I push the dead troll out of my mind and focus on her hand, her incredible hand, beckoning, her palm warm and dry beneath my grateful lips. Their van will be at a motel close by some Atlanta version of Malfunction Junction. I know this because it fits. The dufus will be quick and easy, just like the troll. She will place her hand in mine, tentative at first, then sure. This time, when we escape the embrace of Malfunction Junction, we'll be together.

It all fits.

Yard Sale

"Use that money you hid in the closet, dipshit." The accompanying blow lacked the force to addle, just a glancing upward-sweeping strike to the back of her head. The slap flipped her hair over her face, leaving her flushed and disoriented behind a brown untrimmed tumble. It was Tote's favorite way of reminding Lugene of her standing in his scheme of things.

Lugene had deluded herself into believing that, this time, her mayonnaise jar stash of quarters and dollar bills was adequately hidden. Not so. Not even burying her treasure in a basket of soiled underwear overdue for the laundromat could deter Tote when he was bent on finding. Lugene used both hands to emerge, parting her hair in the middle and tucking it behind her ears. She took a breath to calm her color. "Tip money won't be enough." A protest about his going through her dirty clothes would only bring a second hit, one with knuckles in it.

"Bull shit. Go to the Goodwill or something."

Which Lugene did, except not the Goodwill. She'd noticed a yard sale within walking distance of the garage apartment she'd rented for the two of them after Tote finished his three-to-five with no time off for anything. Rented by lying to the landlady that her man was getting out of the army.

Janelle's yard sale provided all that Lugene needed. A Gucci clutch, once presented by a smiling grandson to his mamaw, along with the assurance that where the government was sending him was not dangerous. It remained enshrouded in its thick plastic wrapping, thirty years in the dresser atop which she displayed his photograph with a black ribbon across one corner. Janelle had bought the dresser at an estate sale, had allowed herself to once again entertain notions of staying put, accumulating furniture, living better than a furnished rental. The dresser had been a package deal, its lavender-scented contents included in the price. Now, the dresser and the purse and the assortment of old-lady clothes were offered to passersby. Had Janelle known the purse's true pedigree, not doubted that someone on the fixed-income edge of poverty would own a genuine Gucci handbag, she might've held it back.

A plum-colored ensemble of skirt and jacket, worn three times honky-tonking. Janelle had overlooked the unevenness of cut and stitch, thought the outfit right for her job, less so for smoky beer joints. Terry had reminded her that he'd paid for the outfit and she would by God wear it going out with him. On the other hand, Terry accepted that, along with a man's rights came responsibilities. He'd touched her heart when he brought in his toolbox, unasked, and fixed her washing machine. Too bad but maybe lucky too, that repair job led to her doing his laundry, which led to her turning out his pockets and finding a phone number on the back of a diesel fuel receipt. She dialed the number, then bounced the telephone off the wall. The next day, she piled the skirt and jacket on a card table in her front yard, along with the contents of the dresser. She got a neighbor to help her drag the dresser to the yard. Furniture was just another kind of clutter to be eliminated from her life.

A pair of low-heeled shoes, scuffed white, recently borne with tears through the front door of a funeral parlor to be included in the last rites garb of a dear departed. The funeral director had been reassuring and had passed the shoes to the back room where the paying patrons never go. There, a clean-up man smelling of embalming fluid, sure of going undetected because no-one looks to see if a corpse is shod, had bartered the shoes out the back door along with a pair of red cowboy boots, receiving a six-pack in trade. The boots soon graced the feet of a man who'd never been west of the Mississippi but the white shoes ended up being tossed over Janelle's backyard fence. Only the fact that this happened the night before the yard sale kept the shoes from the refuse heap.

All these things Lugene got for nine dollars. She tried on the jacket and discovered that it was two sizes too large but she figured it and the matching skirt were appropriate for the look she needed and paid six dollars without haggling. The shoes were offered for fifty cents because they had a lot of Sunday School miles on them and no one would have paid a dollar. Janelle wanted five dollars for the like-new purse but agreed to two-fifty when Lugene pointed out that it was covered with little G's and her initials were LW and anyway she only had nine dollars.

Lugene donned her new ensemble as soon as she got home. She found Tote at the refrigerator, looking for a beer that wasn't there. He ran his eyes over her. "This is your notion of looking respectable? A suit that don't fit, wore-out shoes, and a purse with somebody else's initials on it? Shit." Tote slammed the refrigerator door. "I need you to look like a bank customer, not a bag lady."

Lugene shrugged. "It's all I had money for."

"Where'd you get this shit?"

"Yard sale."

"I saw it. Some gal trying to sell what oughta be throwed away. I guess she sure saw you coming. Thing is, I told you Goodwill. Rich folks give good stuff to the Goodwill." Tote nodded toward the kitchen table. "Sit down. We better go over this again." He took the chair opposite hers and launched into his solution for all the bad hands he'd been dealt.

Lugene barely listened while Tote plodded through the plan. Most of her mind considered the clothes she'd just put on. The suit was too big—she'd had to tailor the waist with safety pins to keep the skirt from falling down—but she wanted to wear it anyway. Despite its softness, it was sturdy stuff, a fabric that would hold together. Inside it, she felt some security. The shoes needed polish, the old-fashioned chalky white liquid kind, but the depressions in the inner soles fit Lugene's feet perfectly. She'd spent enough ten-hour shifts rushing from kitchen to booth to value good-fitting shoes.

She told herself the purse was the best-made she'd ever owned. Every seam was tight and perfectly straight. As for the G, maybe she could let go of Lugene Wagner. Maybe Gloria Gibbs. With a made-up mother who served iced tea in cut glass and never pulled a night shift. Maybe a father who said grace over supper and never wanted to play the secret game. The suit gave her substance. The shoes gave her ease. The purse gave her style and a dream. She saw no point in trying to explain that to Tote.

"Now tell it back to me."

"I go in, say I want to see the manager. I won't talk to nobody else. I drop the note, he picks it up. He gives me the money. I leave." Lugene looked directly at Tote. "You're waiting in the car. Right?"

"Right around the corner with the engine running."

"I'd feel a lot better if you came in with me."

Tote slammed his hands down on the kitchen table. He lowered his head and shook it several times, then bugged his eyes out so she'd feel his exasperation. "That's the beauty of it, dipshit. You go in when there's other people in the bank.

The note says there's a man with a gun in the lobby. They don't know which one. They play it safe, give you the money. You're gone before they figure out there ain't nobody else." Tote leaned back and raised his hands, palms up. "We're on the interstate while they're chasing their tails inside the bank. Slick."

"What if there's a guard?"

"These small branches around Birmingham ain't got guards. I checked that out."

"What about cameras?"

Again, Tote had a ready answer. "They might, but so what? Nobody knows who you are. I'm the one might get recognized, but I won't be in the bank."

"What if they won't give me any money?"

"They will. They won't die for insured money."

At the bank, Janelle stood behind the high marble counter, rearranging her currency so that all the heads pointed in the same direction. She was planning another yard sale. The last one had been cut short by an afternoon rain right after the mousy little woman bought Terry's suit. She'd taken the remaining clothes inside but left the heavy dresser in the yard. That had been a mistake. It warped and ended up awaiting the trash man. Now, she had to do another yard sale and decide what to do with herself. A bank teller could always get a job, it was just a question of when or where. The why was set. There Terry had been, on Sunday afternoon, right there in Sears in all his disloyal glory, trying to look at a socket set on sale while his latest pouted and sighed and tugged at his arm.

As soon as Lugene came in the front door, Janelle remembered the sharp features, the back-braided hair, the brown eyes that darted around like they were used to watching out. She noted that Lugene looked paler this time but knew that the bank lights sometimes caused that. Then, her eyes swept over Lugene's clothes and confirmed the recognition.

Janelle hoped Lugene would not choose her window, would spare them both a possible embarrassment. She half-formed a plan to step away from her station, but Lugene was moving quickly, weaving through the other customers and boring in on Janelle. Before Janelle could escape, Lugene was at her window.

"Where's the manager?" The question crossed the marble countertop as Lugene recognized Janelle. Each blushed at knowing the other. Janelle forced a smile but Lugene did not. Instead, she blinked and repeated her question.

Janelle knew managers did not want to be bothered with petty questions. Major accounts, maybe. Uneasy women wearing ill-fitting clothes, no way. "May I help you?"

"I got to see the manager. Now."

Janelle also knew that denying such requests could result in a ruckus in the lobby, something managers wished to avoid even if they had to deal with people unable to balance their checkbook. She pointed at a glassed-in cubicle in one corner of the lobby. "Over there." She watched Lugene walk away and hoped the suit had looked better on her.

The manager felt like he'd already had enough aggravation from Janelle for one day. She had fiddled around until his coffee was cold by the time she brought it to him. Now, he glanced through the transparent panels that enclosed him and saw Janelle point in his direction. A somewhat disheveled woman clutching what was surely a fake Gucci purse was following Janelle's directions. Small overdraft, most likely. Still, she'd gotten past the gatekeeper and must be dealt with. She pecked at his door and he waved her in. "Yes?"

Lugene stopped about seven feet from the manager's desk. "I need you to look at this."

The manager held out his hand. He expected the usual,

a statement with some entries circled in pencil. After a few minutes, she'd admit that there could've been more than one withdrawal that day. She'd apologize and he'd send her back to Janelle. Later, he'd chastise Janelle for not heading her off. Janelle had seemed somewhat distracted lately. Distracted was not good in the banking business.

Lugene dropped the note on the floor. She stood stark still.

The manager was always polite to ladies, even peculiar-looking ones who couldn't add up a column of numbers. He stood, stepped away from his desk, picked up the note, and turned back toward his desk.

"Don't go back to your desk. Read it here."

"What?"

"Just read it."

The manager knew two things. He knew what the note would say and he knew that the alarm button was on the underside of his desk. He unfolded the note and read it. He looked out at the lobby. There were several customers in the bank. He read the note again. "No."

"What do you mean, no?"

"Just no. Get out of here."

"He'll shoot you."

"The man with a gun? Please look out the window, lady."

Lugene scanned the lobby, her eyes skipping from customer to customer. Two things Tote had assumed. First, the manager would be more frightened of a gun in a man's hands. Second, some of the customers would be men. The only male in the bank was the manager. All of the tellers and all of the customers were women.

"Get out. If you're lucky, you'll get away before the cops get here."

Lugene backed toward the manager's door, bumped against the jamb, stumbled into the lobby, hurried toward the front door. At the same time, the manager leapt to his desk and pressed the alarm button. The signal reached the police alarm board before Lugene reached the sidewalk.

Lugene rounded the corner and stopped. This was where Tote had let her off. This was where he was supposed to be waiting, hunched over the steering wheel and gunning the engine of his so-called classic El Camino. This was where he had in fact been, sweating and creating noise and smoke, until the black-and-white pulled in behind him and spooked him into driving away. Lugene stared at the policeman bent over the newspaper dispenser. The policeman paid her no heed but came up straight when his radio blared out an alert about a bank robbery in progress. He turned toward Lugene and would have passed her on his way to the bank, except that the manager charged around the corner and shouted, "You're here. That's her."

The policeman had stopped for a newspaper because the sergeant had promised that his name would be in an article along with the other newly hired patrolmen. He had no expectation whatsoever of experiencing, compressed into a few seconds, a call to action, a wild-eyed bank robber clutching a purse and looking for a way to run, and a red-faced man shouting at him and pointing at the woman. The policeman dropped his hand onto the grip of his service pistol.

The following Saturday, Janelle sat up a card table and displayed her remaining wares. Midmorning, a bright yellow El Camino with primer spots on its fenders stopped at the curb. Janelle studied the man who emerged from the car. She rocked back slightly on her heels, crossed her arms, and watched him semi-swagger across her little patch of rented lawn. Too many cowboy movies, she decided, more John Wayne than Clint Eastwood, with that somewhat off-balance forward lurch. She wondered how much time he'd spent, pacing back and forth in some grungy apartment, perfecting his gun-slinger walk. Had he done it in front of a mirror?

Janelle ran her eyes up and down him, even exchange for his doing the same to her. Jeans that could stand on their own. A skinny torso that thickened toward the middle and was in no way flattered by the sleeveless black tee shirt he wore. A gold cross dangling from a strip of rawhide looped around his neck. The strings of muscle running down his long arms implied that he had once done some hard work or pumped some iron, but the paunch behind his oversized belt buckle hinted that the effort had not been recent. He was carrying a plastic bag, swinging it back and forth to imply that its contents had weight and worth and would justify his being there.

Janelle's estimate of when he would turn on the grin was right on target. Ten feet from her display table, he opened his face from ear to ear, a flash of bashfulness and nonchalance with more than a little leer shining through. Janelle held her face immobile and waited for his pitch. There was always a pitch. She'd not make it easy for him.

"I see you got another yard sale going."

Janelle nodded. Maybe silence would erode his confidence in his charms.

It did. "What I mean is, my woman got some stuff from you a month ago."

His woman. Janelle kept her arms crossed and her jaw set. "No returns."

"I wasn't thinking exactly return. Maybe we could go halves. You sell it, we split what you get." He lifted his bag toward Janelle. When she did not take it, he upended it over her table of assorted clothes and kitchen gadgets. Out fell a pair of scuffed white shoes and a new-looking Gucci handbag. On top of them fell a plum-colored skirt. "I guess you recognize this stuff."

Janelle was unable to stifle her sudden intake of breath but Tote did not react to it. She looked him over again, quickly. No place in that getup to hide a gun. He seemed more inclined toward convincing than threatening. "I recognize it. Don't she want it?" It was not a question that needed an answer. Janelle had watched from inside the bank while the bagged body was loaded into the ambulance, seen the thoroughly stricken rookie cop being escorted by his watch commander to another vehicle.

"Naw. She don't need it. She left me but I got her stuff."

Janelle took another look at the bag's exposed contents. "Where's the jacket for the suit?"

"Accident." He lowered his voice. "Had blood on it." He ducked his head. "I throwed it away."

Janelle tasted something bitter rising within her. "Leave it here. I'll do what I can."

Tote nodded. "Thanks. I'll drop by tomorrow." He paused halfway through turning to leave. "Looks like you and me are both kind of on our own. We oughta take whatever this stuff brings and go out, get to know each other."

"I don't know." Terry would have handled it better. No acting like he knew some secret about her. Just a straight-forward invitation to go get something to eat. No expecting her to pay her own way.

Tote restored his grin. "Sure you do, darlin'. You and me, we'll go good together. See ya tomorrow."

Janelle barely waited until he was out of sight. She gathered up her yard sale offerings, carted everything inside, and shoved all of her merchandise into a garbage can. All but the purse. This time, she'd keep it. She called Greyhound and asked about a one-way ticket to California.

Dump Birds

Jack awoke with Charleé on his mind. He wondered if that meant she was thinking about him but decided it did not. He let his feet drop from his desk to the floor, creating enough leverage to lift him from his chair. The nap had only added grogginess to his shakes. He rocked, established a semblance of equilibrium and focus, found the pint of bourbon adrift amongst the student-generated detritus littering his cubicle. He tossed back a shot of eye-opener, shuddered, held the bottle up to the light seeping through the blinds. Little remained so he drained the bottle. Revived, he snatched up his notes, unlatched his office door, propelled himself down the corridor toward his classroom. He kept score. No eye contact, two. Brief nod, one. Scurry around a corner, one. Jack's colleagues knew about his Mondays.

Jack's World Civilization students, his diminishing collection of hairdressers-in-training and welders-to-be, awaited him in abject somnolence. Although they were in their fourth month together a few still glanced around when he arrived, momentarily titillated. The total Jack was a discordant montage of professorial goatee, cheap western-style boots, beltless slacks, stained shirt, yellow-tinted eyeglasses forced on him by an aberrant gene.

He glanced at his notes, dropped them onto the lectern, began pacing. He lectured to a space above his students' heads, parsed the grandeur of Rome. Halfway into his allotted fifty minutes he continued his hoarse monotone but dropped his gaze and scanned the room. Kristi, the terminally distracted daughter of a greyhound breeder, was attempting to capture the dust motes in the late April sunshine slanting across the West Florida Technical College classroom. Corey and the ballplayer whose name he never remembered were sharing a snicker while their hands dove between their respective thighs to adjust and cradle. Shaneeka, no doubt awake past midnight responding to fries-to-go or an infant's wail, was napping.

Jack continued to list the legacies of Rome while he drifted closer to the whispering athletes. He felt the gorge rising from the turbulent pool of bourbon and doughnuts in his gut. He paused in front of his prospective victims and gauged the angle and distance. He could catch both in one spew. Corey and his teammate exchanged silent glances and placed their hands flat on their desks. Jack studied his watch. It was Charleé time. "See you Wednesday."

In previous incarnations, Cabaret Charleé had been a filling station and, more recently, the temple of a hellfire-and-brimstone preacher. The preacher, before he decided to put his knowledge of sin to better profit and moved to Miami to open an adult book store, tore out the gas pumps and added a cinder-block extension to the back of the building. Charleé brought in an assortment of potted palms and ferns and a jukebox featuring Golden Oldies. She placed wrought-iron tables where oil additives once were displayed and a glass-topped bar where the altar had been. Despite its lingering aromas of axle grease and sweaty piety the cabaret became a popular destination for a variety of drinkers.

Jack claimed his usual seat at the bar, away from the sunlight and near the men's room. He waited, his shoulders squeezed together and down to dampen the roiling within, while Charleé finished a primp. Charleé knew makeup, the subtle emphasis of a good feature, the expert obscuring of a wrinkle just beginning to insinuate itself. She was equally careful with clothing, choosing boldly feminine blouses that artfully draped her lean, athletic figure. Jack requested his standard hard-day remedy. "Double Beam, Bud back."

Charleé tossed a tastefully frosted tress away from her eyes. With one manicured hand she easily lifted a bottle from the bar well and tilted it to a double shot glass. With a voice that hinted of Tabasco and unfiltered cigarettes she greeted Jack. "How's it going?"

Jack's rigid forefinger thumped twice on the bartop. "Better if I had a drink."

She sat the glass of whiskey and a frosted mug of beer in front of her only mid-afternoon customer. She turned her back to Jack and busied herself with barmistress tasks. She'd answer the rough taunts of motorcycle couples with a laugh as hearty as theirs. She'd reward the stares of sailors from Whiting Field with a sashay of her tight derrière. But she'd made it an unswerving practice never to respond to anger. Not even from Jack would she take that.

Jack chugged his whiskey and gulped half of his beer. "Sorry. Didn't mean to take it out on you." He finished his beer and clinked his glass against his mug.

Charleé responded to Jack's signal. Then, she placed her hands on the bar and considered Jack through the green contact lenses she inserted every morning. "What's wrong?"

Jack knocked back his second whiskey and took a sip of beer. "Nothing. Just another day trying to coax the darkened souls of the sweltering masses into the light of learning. It's never gonna happen, you know."

Charleé softened her voice. "I know it happened with me. I couldn't run this place and go to college without you tutoring me."

"You're one in a thousand." Jack drained his mug and paid his tab. "Call me later."

On his way home Jack stopped at the Piggly Wiggly. He glanced at a variety of frozen dinners but chose a package of fish sticks and another of au gratin potatoes. He studied the labels of the California jug wines but settled for a six-pack of on-sale beer. He drove across Raybun, watched for the town's policeman, hurried to finish a can of beer, pulled into his driveway.

In the kitchen, Jack opened a second beer. He stashed the remainder of the six-pack in the refrigerator—just enough for breakfast. He ripped open the package of fish sticks, grimaced, tossed it and the potatoes into the freezer. Beer in hand, he strolled into the living room. Sprawled on the couch next to a bachelor clutter of half-read magazines and unfolded laundry, he punched the Play button on the telephone answering machine. Charleé invited him to return her call. He sat up and punched in the memorized number. "Jack here. Sure, happy to. Your place? Oh. Okay. No, it's no problem." Jack drained his can of beer and headed toward the front door.

Jack returned to the Piggly Wiggly. He considered Cabaret Charleé but a fumble through his wallet turned up twenty dollars to cover several hours' drinking and a hoped-for dinner with Charleé. A six-pack cost less than two drinks at the bar. He opted for quantity over quality.

He then killed three hours, limited himself to four beers, enough to keep his nerves deadened but not end up totally sloshed. He took to the long stretches of Panhandle blacktop that extend in straight lines to the pine woods of Alabama. They were roads he knew well, a Florida never featured in

Visitors Bureau videos, a Florida without margaritas or palm trees. To pay his way at the nondescript public colleges he'd attended after he got out of the navy, Jack had patrolled these roads for more than twelve years. He'd rooted out Ma and Pa Cracker, practiced the one-call close, gulled them into buying aluminum siding or burial policies or poster-size photos of their grandchildren. No money down. Easy payments from now on.

Near the Alabama line Jack turned onto a dirt road marked by a hand-lettered sign urging him to *Dump Here*. Others inclined to accept the invitation had come and gone earlier in the day. He was alone except for the flies and the birds. The birds were large and mostly white. Seabirds up from the Gulf on a shopping trip, he assumed. He reached beneath the seat and withdrew the revolver he'd bought from a student desperate to finance a night at a rave in Pensacola. He finished the beer he'd been nursing and exited his car.

Jack watched a cluster of six birds. They were busy with a sack of kitchen garbage. They'd already ripped the plastic bag open and were engaged in plucking potato peels from amongst empty tomato cans and soiled paper towels. He recognized the birds for what they were, strutting scavengers, arrogant in their stupidity, picking over that which was once of some worth. They deserved to be reminded of their place in the order of things and their kind could only understand violence.

That suited Jack just fine. He lifted the heavy pistol, cocked it, fired. He missed the bird he'd aimed at but took another broadside. The .45 caliber slug dislodged several feathers and sent the stricken bird tumbling. The other birds screamed in outrage and beat their way aloft. One made a half-hearted feint toward Jack. Two snapped shots missed their mark but ended the bird's brief show of courage. He executed a flapping pivot and fled to the safety of the flock.

Jack stood still. Greed would ultimately trump fear. After scarcely a minute the birds returned to pecking at filth. This time, Jack hit the one he aimed at. The survivors fled to the far side of the dump and remained there. Jack let the pistol hang by his side and strolled to the edge of the garbage pit. He evacuated the result of an afternoon of drinking, added yellow to the red staining the carcass of his first victim. He zipped himself up, wiped his hand on his trousers, returned to his car, placed the revolver on the seat beside him.

Jack organized his meandering so that, at the agreed-upon time, he was at the Woolesley campus. Perched on what passed for a hill in essentially flat Florida, Woolesley College was twenty-eight miles and a world away from Raybun and WestTech. Jack sometimes informed his students that Woolesley boasted half the student body and twice the cumulative intelligence quotient of WestTech. He passed beneath one of the guardian arches at the edge of the stately amalgam of brick and magnolias, took the route that led past the fraternity houses, sensed and hated the smell and pulse of money and tradition.

Jack parked in the visitors' lot. He ate a handful of breath mints while he walked to the library. Charleé was waiting in the well-lit lobby on a leather couch next to a boy ten years her junior. They both rose. Charleé smiled. Her companion gave Jack a once-over and grinned.

"Dr. Freeman, this is Wade. We're in French together."

Jack gripped Wade's hand, stepped close, exhaled an almost-visible miasma of stale beer. "Pleased to meet you, Wade."

Wade leaned back but retained his grin. "Me too, sir." He rescued his hand and placed it on the back of Charleé's neck. "Gotta go. Chapter meeting. See ya later."

"Bye." Charleé waited until Wade was ten steps away, then turned to Jack. "You okay?"

"Absolutely copacetic."

"I take it you continued to relax after you left my place."

"Marx is easier to take with a buzz. Let's do it."

Jack and Charleé found a table tucked among the stacks. After nearly an hour of dialectic materialism, interrupted by Jack's trips to the rest room and the water cooler, he reached across the table and closed Charleé's book. "That's enough of this crap for now."

Charleé wove her fingers together, palms outward, and stretched. "So, what's been eating you all day?"

Jack broke eye contact with Charleé. He looked over her shoulder at the dull reds, blues, and browns of FAA to FEN. "Call it dissatisfaction with my station in life. I envy your freedom."

"Jack, if I'm free to be myself so are you."

Jack shifted his gaze to FOR, to a book that was taller than most and bright green. "I want more than WestTech. I want—" He sorted through his brain for a satisfying word but found none. "A great passion. And someone to share it with." He glared at the impertinent book. "I sound like a damn fool."

Charleé laid a light hand on Jack's. "Your great passion is teaching. You share that with me."

He turned his hand so that he could curl his fingers around hers. "At least we have that." He released her hand before she could withdraw it and began stacking her books. "I need something to eat. You want a barbecue and a beer?"

"No thanks. Wade's going to bring a pizza over to my apartment."

The flush of Jack's face darkened. "Wade. What's with you and that kid?"

"He's my school-girl crush. I'm his older woman adventure. He's sweet."

"He know about Charlie?"

"Charlie is history, Jack. Who I tell is my business."

"I just don't want you to get hurt."

"I appreciate that. Maybe I'll tell Wade about Charlie when the time is right."

Jack pushed his chair back and spoke as he rose. "I guess it's time to go."

Charleé smiled, picked up her books, stood. "Okay. Thanks as always."

"You want to study again tomorrow?"

"Wade's going to help me with French."

"Well, call me if you want to."

"Thanks again." Charleé walked ahead of Jack to the elevator.

Jack parked in the lot of the Home Folks Barbecue. He got out of his car, stepped to the counter, recognized one of his students. "Evening, Brandi. Two inside lean to go."

A second customer got out of her car, a silver Volvo station wagon, and spoke to Jack. "Dr. Freeman."

Jack turned. "Dean Archer. Good evening."

"Good evening." Dean Archer requested a small Diet Coke. "Jack, I need to speak with you tomorrow. It will be formal so you should begin gathering your thoughts."

Jack peered into the dean's determinedly neutral face. "About what?"

Dean Archer removed her glasses and rubbed the bridge of her nose. "Two more of your World Civilization students have withdrawn. That leaves, what, seven out of twenty-three?"

"Basketball players?"

"Yes, actually."

Jack received his order from Brandi. "They'll flunk if they withdraw now."

Dean Archer nodded. "I reminded them but that's not the crux of the issue." She cleared her throat. "They offered some observations about your habit of letting class out early and heading for your favorite bar. The president, as you know, has some strict ideas about that."

"You're going to the president with this?"

"Dr. Freeman, as your dean I feel obliged to report a problem of this nature."

Jack hurled his sack of barbecue at the dean, missed her but left a splat of barbecue sauce on the window. "Fuck you, fuck the president, fuck WestTech." He took a breath. "Fuck Wade."

Dean Archer pleaded with Brandi to let her call the police. As he got into his car, Jack saw that Brandi had placed a telephone on the counter and the dean was making her report. She was waving her free hand in an effort to convey the urgency of the matter. Brandi waved goodbye to Jack. He nodded to Brandi as he drove away.

On his way home Jack detoured to WestTech. He finished the beer he'd opened during the brief drive, went into the featureless building containing his office. He sat at a desk cluttered with papers he should have graded a week earlier, popped the top of the beer he'd brought with him, began removing things from a desk drawer. A two-year-old West Florida Technical College graduation program listed Charles Robert Carter as an honor graduate. Tucked into the program was a folded note to Dear Dr. Freeman from Charlie the Barkeep. Charlie thanked Jack for three years of tutoring and said he'd be back in about a year and not to give up on him. Next, Jack found a year-old newspaper article featuring a photograph of an attractive woman of about thirty over the announcement that Woolesley College had awarded the Stavros Scholarship to Charleé Reneé Cartiér. Scrawled across the photograph, in the same handwriting as the thank-you note, was "I'm back."

Jack pressed his lips to the black and white image of Charleé. He tore the history of Charlie/Charleé into small pieces and jammed them into an already-full waste basket. He finished his beer, crushed the can, attempted to shove it on top of the shredded keepsakes. The basket was too full and the can fell onto the floor where Jack left it.

Back in his car Jack broke the seal on the emergency pint he kept beneath the front seat. A pint wasn't much but it would have to do. He took a deep breath and forced his memory to focus. The pin on Wade's chest just above his shirt pocket. Pi Delta Pi. Wade would go there after he finished with Charleé. Jack checked the revolver. Two rounds left. Enough.

Dark Dancing

Blind girls' eyes make tears just like normal girls. I learned that before the night ended. Angela's eyes were sunk in but, overall, she had a face like a famous picture. She had real stylish hair, brown and bobbed short. Her skin reminded me of a ceramic doll. She looked like you'd leave a mark if you touched her. Angela was the youngest of the three sisters, not much over twenty.

On the other hand, Addie, my date, was older than me and whistled. Not all the time, but she'd pucker up at any excuse. Soon as she laid eyes on me, her face said, "What'd I do to deserve this?" I wished I had the nerve to say, "Fred here, who I only know because we're on the same shift, has the hots for Annette. She made him bring somebody for you. His friends knew better." Instead, I grinned and shook her hand, which she jerked back as quick as she could.

Annette, the middle sister, was near my age, thirty-one. She served lemonade made from real lemons and giggled a lot for her age.

Angela didn't have a date. I was glad of that. We played cards, used a deck with both pictures and Braille. Angela won the most. Around nine, we took a lemonade break. We got to talking about the race riots that were all over the Birmingham newspapers and television stations. Annette, looking to talk about something else, asked me about my job. I tried to explain how to make steel in an open hearth furnace. Fred kept correcting me, even though he was only a second helper and I was a first.

Then, Addie offered to whistle for us. Before we could say anything, she launched into a medley of show tunes. It wasn't much of a show. She claimed to be a trained whistler but she must've missed some lessons. We all got fidgety but Addie just tootled away. Finally, she had to take a breath and Annette jumped in. Annette declared that Angela was a ballet dancer and a good one, blind or not. "Somebody takes her once around the stage to memorize it and she's ready. They never announce she's blind until the end. Nobody believes it. She even got away with it in New York City."

Angela got rose petals in her cheeks. "I didn't get away with anything, I just didn't let it stop me. The choreographer was more concerned about my lack of experience with a partner."

Dancing's not something I'd ordinarily choose to talk about but this dancing had to do with Angela. "You always dance alone?"

Addie butted in. "Precious doesn't do anything on her own. I help pay for her dance lessons. We know she appreciates it." Annette hissed at the sourpuss to hush. Addie got redder and said, "Well, excuse me." I guess she was ticked off because she'd not finished the show tunes.

Angela ignored the spat and turned toward me. Her eyes went off to nowhere but I didn't care. "My teachers fear a partner will be concerned about my blindness and his style will be hampered. You often do things alone, too, don't you?"

That surprised me. "How can you tell?"

"I'm sorry. I shouldn't intrude. But, everyone else says 'We did something.' You say 'I did something.' I have a bad habit of analyzing people."

I liked being analyzed by a pretty girl. "It's okay. What else can you tell about me?"

"You had onions for supper."

"I guess I should've brushed better."

Little tears came into the corners of her eyes. "I'm sorry again. Maybe that's why I never have a partner."

I let it drop.

Angela had hit the nail on the head. I was a loner. Maybe it had to do with the way I look or the way I'd been raised. For whatever reason, I got left out. One time, I heard some guys at the plant talking about drag racing and it sounded interesting. So, I went to the drag strip. I didn't race, I just watched. The guys from work were there with girls who wore tight shorts and smoked cigarettes and hollered cusswords at the racers. I couldn't fit in with that so I never went back.

Mostly, on my off-days, I'd wash and wax the new Oldsmobile I bought every year, pack a cooler of baloney sandwiches and root beer, and just take off. I'd ride around by myself, back roads all the way down to Montgomery or up to Huntsville. I could look all I wanted to and not be bothered with people looking back.

I tried to call Angela the day after we met. She answered but called Addie to the phone before I could explain I wanted to talk to her. I made a lame excuse about calling to say thanks. It took me two months to get up the nerve to try again. I was on the night shift that week, so I was off while her parents and sisters were at work. I went home, took a nap, got cleaned up, and made it to her door by noontime. "You still dancing by yourself?"

Angela clapped her hands. "Luke."

"You remember me?"

"I recognized your voice."

"You want a cheeseburger?"

Angela pointed her nose toward me and sniffed the way kittens do. "Do you have one?"

"Not on me." She giggled and I caught on. "You're teasing me."

"I'm sorry. I'm such a smart-aleck. Are you inviting me to lunch?"

"Yes."

"Luke, I would love to join you for lunch." She held the door open and waved me into the living room. "I'll slip on something more appropriate."

I checked her out when she left the room. There was nothing wrong with her jeans, dancers have the kind of figures they make jeans for, but I didn't tell her that. She came back in a frilly dress, low-cut just enough, with pink flowers. I was in love before we got out the door.

I was grateful for her blindness, which I've never seen as cruel of me. I didn't wish it on her. She'd been born blind. It was sometimes a problem for her, not driving, reading only in Braille, searching for something in plain sight. But, there was no call for feeling sorry. She got along fine without seeing. She could recognize somebody by a hitch in their gait. She knew what somebody had been doing by their smell—sweat or perfume or food. A tone of voice told her somebody's mood. Angela was in no way needful of pity.

One look at me and you'd understand my being thankful she was blind. I'm short and chunky. My hands are oversized. I started losing my hair the same year I started getting pimples. My nose is flat as a pug dog's. I overheard somebody say that I had a face only a mother could love. Well, mine got sick of looking at me, dumped me in a foster home, and bought a one-way ticket to ride.

We celebrated our three-months-dating anniversary at a ritzy restaurant. I'd never liked places like that, but now I got a kick out of strolling in with Angela on my arm and watching people stare. Going in, she asked me what color flowers they had.

Earlier, she'd got me to call and ask about their best meal. After we were seated, she pretended to study the menu. She told the waiter their pansies were pretty and she'd have the prime rib. It's not that she was ashamed of being blind. She wanted to prove something. It's hard to explain but I felt powerful, being with her. Angela knew how to overcome shortcomings.

Back at her house, we stood on her porch for a minute. "You respect me, don't you, Luke?"

"Yes. Why'd you ask?"

"Because you've never tried to take advantage of me."

This conversation was making me nervous. "I know you're not that kind of girl."

"Luke, even my kind of girl may wish to be kissed by her beau."

She kept her lips pressed together and I did too. It was more of a peck than a kiss. I wanted to do more than that so I put my hands on her cheeks. She made a little gasp and stepped back.

"Did I hurt you?"

"Not exactly. It's just that your hands are bigger and rougher than I expected."

I put my big mitts against my chest, where they'd stay out of trouble. "They've always been that way. From work, I guess."

"It's all right. But that's enough for now, Luke." She was right. Some things are worth waiting for.

Annette married Fred and was okay with Angela marrying me. But Addie decided that what she could see, and Angela couldn't, needed to be brought up. I was so proud of Angela. She told her family that what Addie said about me didn't matter. She said I'd be good to her, like I always had. She said I'd encouraged her to continue dancing, which was true. She said looks don't matter, only the heart, and I had a good heart. Her momma agreed. Her daddy continued to hem and haw for a while but

Angela acted sweet to him. Finally, he gave in and that shut Addie down.

Annette was the maid of honor and right pretty. Addie hunkered down like a bullfrog because Angela wouldn't let her whistle at our wedding. I was stuck with Fred for my best man. We got married in the morning and went to Gulf Shores. Angela chattered about dancing all the way down. I wondered how much she knew about sex. I hoped it was more than what I knew.

What I knew came mostly from my foster parents' church. They were foot-washers and held sex to be Devil-inspired. Its only Christian use was what they called procreation. Sex that wasn't part of having a family, they called fornication. Matter of fact, practically everything a teenage boy might want to do—smoking, drinking, beating off—was sinful. They got me to sign a pledge card not to go to dances or the picture show. But they accepted me, ugly and all. They said I had a beautiful soul and made me a junior deacon.

Living in accordance with the Word of God was mostly not that hard for me. I never had many chances to sin, anyway. Except once. I was fifteen and I got this cockamamie notion to spend the day hitchhiking out into the country. I got several rides and saw a lot of barns and fields but I also got turned around. I ended up standing alongside a road wishing I'd headed home sooner. About then, a jeep with three guys in it went by. They yelled and one gave me the finger. About five minutes later they came back and said they'd take me to Birmingham. I'd been warned about falling in with the likes of them. I could've run into the woods and they probably would've left. But, they were cutting up and saying I was a chicken if I didn't come with them. Besides, it had got almost dark.

They took me to a house on a dirt road and got to shooting dice. Instead of playing for money, they played for me. The winner got to make me do stuff. One turned on a radio and made me dance. I'd never done any dancing so I just shuffled my feet around and jerked my elbows up and down. I felt goofy and scared at the same time. Another made me take a big swig of whatever they were drinking and laughed when I nearly puked.

After that the jeep driver won. He made me take my pants off and wiggle my butt when I danced. Then he made me get down on all fours. He yanked my shorts down. I begged him not to hurt me. He said anybody as ugly as me ought to appreciate the attention. He got what he wanted and then the others took a turn. I thought they'd kill me but they dumped me beside the road when they were through with me.

I kept it to myself for three years, until I heard a sermon about giving up your sins to a forgiving God. So, I went to the youth minister and told him about being poked in the behind. His face got red and he asked me what it felt like. I told him it hurt. The next day, he asked me if I still did it or wanted to. I said I didn't. The day after that, he said it wouldn't be right for me to continue serving the body and blood. I felt so bad, I stopped going to church. Even so, I promised Jesus I'd never again commit the sin of fornication, not listen to people talk about it, not look at pictures of it, nothing. That wasn't an easy promise to keep but I kept it.

Angela got real quiet after we got to our motel. She came out of the bathroom in a flannel nightie and laid down on the bed. I undressed and laid down beside her. I was ready but also nervous about what to do next. So I said, "You know what to do, don't you?"

"I thought it was up to the man to know what to do. I've never done anything."

If I'd quit right then, things later might've turned out different. But, because I had procreation on my mind, I told her to turn over.

"Why?"

"Like you said, it's up to me to know what to do."

I lifted her nightgown. Her bottom looked like two pearls pushed together. I got on top of her and tried to do what I figured I was supposed to. Her body went rigid as a board, then she commenced to scream and kick until I got off. She stumbled to the bathroom and refused to come out until I said I'd sleep in the car. The next morning, we didn't even eat, just packed up and headed back to Birmingham. As soon as we got home, Angela called Sears and ordered furniture for a second bedroom.

Other than three drunks taking their turns at me, I'd done without sex all my life, anyway. A few times, I tried talking to Angela about it. Each time, she'd start yelling about my stupidity and my unnatural desires. Each time, it took her longer to get over it. After a while, I had to face it. I'd brought this on myself, not intentionally, but it was my fault. The Devil can get to you in a lot of ways.

I'd bought a three-bedroom brick house over the mountain, as the nicer area is called. Angela was comfortable around that kind of people, her being in the arts and having a college degree. They were highly impressed by her—everybody always was. I put a lot of effort into our yard, rock paths leading through arbors and beds of yellow jonquils. I also kept my promise about encouraging Angela's dancing. When she said she needed a partner, I said she ought to find one.

"The problem is finding someone with the self-confidence to dance with a blind partner. Someone who won't compensate for so-called handicaps. A lot of trust is required."

"Do you know anybody like that?"

"My teacher does. She's just moved here from New York. My teacher says she worked with blind dancers up there and understands us."

"She?"

"I know. Partners are usually one male, one female. But it doesn't have to be. Men sometimes dance female parts. My teacher says Lucy can dance any part."

I figured this Lucy might make Angela feel better about things in general. "Go for it."

"I shall." She touched her cheek to mine. "Thanks for understanding."

Lucy bought an old fieldstone house in Southside and turned it into a dance studio. Most of her neighbors were university people from India or some such place. Angela made me drop her off and pick her up at the curb. She said this helped establish her independence and increased Lucy's confidence in her. I didn't feel right about that, but I'd learned not to argue with Angela.

Yardwork took over my off-time. The neighbors hardly ever spoke to me, but a couple of them came around when they saw how good my yard looked. Before long, I started doing other people's yards. I liked the yard work, especially the heavy work, which I preferred to do by hand. I could swing a machete with the best of them. My hands kept getting tougher and rougher but I didn't have anybody to touch, anyway. The extra money from my yardwork went toward converting what should've been a baby's room into a dance studio. I did a first-class job, with hardwood floors and those rails dancers practice with.

Angela had a party—she called it a grand opening—for her studio. Her dancer friends tried to be nice, but I caught a couple of them staring at me. Lucy tried the hardest to be polite to me. She offered me her hand, like a man would. She was as slender as Angela but taller. Lucy moved more like an athlete than the boy dancers. I could see her running track. She had a hard jaw and long muscles in her arms.

Lucy was the best-looking colored girl I'd ever seen. Her skin reminded me of coffee with a lot of milk. She had a sharp little nose and regular-size lips, not like the negroes I was used to. Her accent was more yankee than anything else. It was only her color and her kinky hair, which was tight on her skull, that showed what she truly was.

The other thing about Lucy was her hands. She had long, slim fingers and her palms were smooth and pink and pliable. They weren't weak, just soft. When we shook, her hand disappeared into mine but she gave me a good grip. She looked straight into my eyes and said her name was Zaire.

After she took her hand back, I could still feel the warmth and the softness. It was the first time I'd ever shook hands with a negro, male or female. The union had gone along with hiring a few for low level jobs in the plant, but I hardly ever spoke to those. The only negro women I'd been around were waitresses. Ordering a barbecue doesn't require handshaking.

My face got hot. "Oh. I thought she danced with somebody named Lucy."

"Didn't Angela tell you? I've exchanged my slave name for one reflecting my heritage. My people were abducted from Africa to the Caribbean to Virginia." Lucy, Zaire, whoever, put her hand on my shoulder and kind of smiled. "This is all very new for you. The important thing is, I love Angela."

That's not something I wanted to hear from some highfalutin colored girl. But this was not the time and place to make a fuss about it. "Yeah. Everybody does."

Zaire nodded. "True. She's a remarkable woman and a remarkable dancer."

"She says you're a good partner."

"*Somos muy simpatico.*"

I'd heard Spanish before but I didn't know they spoke it in Africa. Art people like to show off but I could remind myself that I made more money than most of them.

Angela pretended she didn't want to when the others asked them to dance, but Zaire grinned like a pretty possum. Zaire said they'd do this interpretative number they'd been working on, called A to Z. A tinkerbell boy sat down at the piano I'd bought for the studio and the show commenced. I watched Zaire lift Angela above her head, jack her up as good as any man could've. Then, Zaire let Angela's body slide down her own. Angela quivered all the way down. I overheard a girl dancer whisper that this was the shock of first encounter. They took turns touching each other all over with their fingertips. I guessed that showed them getting acquainted. They wrapped their arms and legs around each other and swayed back and forth. The girl dancer said the message was black and white joining through lovers' consummation. By the time A and Z collapsed in a sweaty pile on the floor, I understood what was sinful about dancing.

I saved what needed to be said until the next morning. "Do you understand what she is?"

Angela swallowed a bite of yogurt. "I assume you mean Zaire?"

"Whatever she calls herself. Maybe dance people don't care, but this is still Alabama."

"Care about what?"

"Zaire is a negro. She had her hands all over you." I played my trump card. "Your parents wouldn't like that."

Angela slammed her yogurt down on the table. "My family also disapproved of you, Luke. Zaire and I use our art to express universal feelings. We're dancers, for God's sake."

I didn't know much about art, but I knew how I felt about Zaire rubbing herself against Angela. Maybe it wasn't fornication, but it was something like it. I also knew that, if I said any more, Angela would pitch a bigger fit. "I'm going to work."

"Fine. By the way, the correct term is Afro-American."

Angela practically disappeared during the weeks before their first dance show. She said her own studio didn't provide the freedom of movement they needed, so she took to spending a lot of time at Zaire's. I continued to take her over there and pick her up until Zaire started coming to get her. Sometimes I didn't know where Angela was, what with me working two jobs and her dancing every day and sleeping in her own bedroom. I didn't fuss about it because Angela looked tired all the time and was a ball of nerves.

I was watching a late movie when the phone rang. It was Angela. To tell the truth, I thought she was asleep in her room. I know it bothered her to send me into her room, but she needed a certain pair of dancing slippers. She'd forgotten them and Zaire was too tired to come get them. She told me to go straight to her closet, find the shoes, and bring them to Zaire's.

Blind people can be as messy as normal people. Angela's room looked like it'd exploded. I guess she couldn't find something and got upset. The only thing not messed up was her bed, which hadn't been slept in. I stepped over a pile of girl stuff and found her shoes in the closet.

I don't know what caused me to snoop around. It's not my usual nature. Maybe I thought her sending me in there made it okay. On her dresser was a little brown bottle with black designs on it. I pulled the stopper out and took a whiff. I guess it was perfume but it had an odd, musty smell. I picked up some undies she'd thrown on the floor. They were white and lacy and I held them against my face. They had the same musty smell, only stronger. That smell made me think about procreation and I felt myself start to get hard. I took one more sniff, then folded the panties and put them on the corner of Angela's bed.

I figured I better get over to Zaire's but then a recording tape partly under her bed caught my eye. There was a tape player on the dresser. I threaded the tape onto the machine and punched Play. Angela's voice gave the title of the poem. *Hard Hands, Soft Hands.* I listened to it all the way through. Then, I put it back under her bed and got out of there.

Angela was waiting at Zaire's door. She held her hand out for the shoes. "That took long enough." She grabbed the shoes when I touched them to her hand and started to close the door.

"You want me to wait for you?"

"Zaire will bring me home. We may have to practice all night."

"Zaire's too tired to fetch your slippers but not too tired to dance all night?"

"Fetch? There's a fine old Southern tradition. Give me a break." She slammed the door.

The mayor of Birmingham and three TV stations came to their opening night. The newspapers ran a front-page story about Birmingham growing in racial togetherness. There was a picture of Angela and Zaire draped all over each other. Over the picture was a headline, "A and Z Raise Money for Multicultural Center." One night, some rednecks stood in the back and booed. They were drowned out by the standing ovation and the cops ran them off.

After their show closed, I told Angela she should spend some time with her momma, who saw her even less than I did. It surprised her that I was concerned about her mother but she liked the idea. I drove her to her parents' house. Angela and her momma got to chatting about the good old days. I said I had to do a yard and left.

I had to tell Zaire twice who I was when she answered her telephone. But, she understood about Angela being down in the dumps over their show ending. She agreed to come over and cheer her up. I said I had to do a yard pretty soon and they could spend some time together. She asked to speak to Angela but I said she was in the shower and to come on over. For once, I didn't feeling nervous, just kind of empty.

When I opened the door for Zaire, she had that know-it-all smile I remembered from before. I hadn't been sure of what to do until right then. I said Angela was still in the bathroom and asked Zaire to sit at the kitchen table and hold my whetstone while I sharpened my machete. She gave me a big-eyed look but she did it, held it with both hands on the table. Give credit where it's due, Zaire was not the kind to back away from something that would scare most negroes.

The machete took Zaire's hands off at the wrist, sliced right through flesh and bone, both hands at the same time. Zaire never moved nor made a sound. Shock, I guess.

I'd lied about getting ready to go do a yard, I was actually on my way to the plant for the afternoon shift. I wrapped her hands in aluminum foil and put them in a paper bag and took them with me. I left Zaire sitting there, staring at a whetstone in a pool of blood, waiting for Angela to finish her long shower. I told Zaire I'd be back in a little while.

At the plant, I waited until nobody was paying attention, strolled over to the furnace, and tossed in what looked like my lunch. There was a puff of flame for not even a second. I told my boss I felt sick and he said I could leave. On my way home to take care of the body, I got to remembering Zaire's soft, warm hand in mine. After a few minutes I told myself, "What's done is done."

An ambulance was pulling away and three cop cars were in front of our house. They had me before I could turn around. In court, Angela said she and her momma had got to fussing at one another and she'd insisted her momma drive her home. Angela entered the house alone. The smell of blood led her to the kitchen. She recognized her visitor by touching her face. She said she was hysterical for a while after she touched Zaire's stumps, then she called 911.

By the time the prosecutor finished, everybody in Alabama knew about how my brutal perversions drove my poor wife into a relationship with the woman I murdered in cold blood. The prosecutor said I was racially motivated. He said Birmingham had been too long under the influence of the Klan. He said it was not only a beautiful, talented dancer who'd died, it was understanding and tolerance.

My lawyer got worried and put me on the stand to say I'd never held with the Klan. I told the jury the negroes never did me any harm and I'd never looked to harm any of them. That gave the prosecutor a shot. He got me to say that negroes would be better off in their own place. The jury, half of it negro women, sat there and nodded and made up their minds. Nobody, including me, was surprised when it took the jury exactly nine minutes to find me guilty. I expected the chair but didn't get it.

After they took me to prison, Angela sold the house and furniture. She moved in with her parents and gave Addie my last Oldsmobile. I've been told she quit dancing, which is unfortunate.

The day I got processed in, a spade sporting an afro issued me my duds. He spit in my face and said I'd have my butt busted wide open and an ice pick in my liver inside of a week. I knew he meant it—even though, setting aside the fact I did kill one of them, I'd never been a racist. I'd always been careful to call them negroes and not niggers. But, in the penitentiary, it's black there and white here and dog eat dog. You're part of it, like it or not. Lucky for me, the Aryan Nation guys acted like I was a white hero. That was a load of crap. I've got no use for them, either. But, it protected me from being shanked by the black boys. Nothing I'd ever learned in church had that power.

After awhile, some fresh meat came in. The white cons fell in love with a skinny young guy with wavy hair and an earring. The blacks got into a tussle over who owned this fat kid who squealed every time somebody poked him. All that ruckus got their attention away from me. I'm grateful for that. I've seen them fornicating, one hunched over the other, humping away like the sinful mutts they are. It reminds me of all that I'll be held to account for in eternity.

JIMMY CARL HARRIS enlisted in the Marines after graduating from high school and worked his way up to the rank of Sergeant Major. During those years, he fought in two wars and earned two degrees from Chapman College. Upon retirement from the military, he completed a doctorate at the University of Alabama. While an Assistant Professor at Southeastern Louisiana University, he authored articles for professional journals. Now retired from academia, he writes fiction full-time. He currently resides in Birmingham, Alabama.

For more information about Jimmy Carl Harris visit:
www.jimmycarlharris.com

Printed in the United States
50840LVS00002B/487-534